EX LIBRIS

VINTAGE **CLASSICS**

THE ASCENT OF RUM DOODLE

Led by the reliably under-insightful Binder, a team of seven British men including Dr Prone (constantly ill); Jungle the route finder (constantly lost), Constant the diplomat (constantly arguing) and 3,000 Yogistani porters, set out to conquer the highest peak in the Himalayas. An outrageously funny spoof about the ascent of a 40,000-and-a-half-foot peak, *The Ascent of Rum Doodle* has been a cult favourite since its publication in 1956.

W.E. BOWMAN

W.E. Bowman (1912-85) was a civil engineer who spent his free time hill-walking, painting and writing (unpublished) books on the Theory of Relativity. He was married with two children

W.E. BOWMAN

The Ascent of Rum Doodle

WITH AN INTRODUCTION BY
Bill Bryson

VINTAGE

1 3 5 7 9 10 8 6 4 2

Vintage
20 Vauxhall Bridge Road
London SW1V 2SA

Vintage is part of the Penguin Random House group of companies
whose addresses can be found at global.penguinrandomhouse.com

Penguin
Random House
UK

First published by Max Parrish & Co Ltd in 1956
First published in Vintage in 2010
This edition published by Vintage in 2019

penguin.co.uk/vintage

A CIP catalogue record for this book is available from
the British Library

ISBN 9781784875299

Printed and bound in Great Britain by Clays Ltd, Elcograf S.p.A.

Penguin Random House is committed to a sustainable future for
our business, our readers and our planet. This book is made
from Forest Stewardship Council® certified paper.

MIX
Paper from
responsible sources
FSC
www.fsc.org
FSC® C018179

Contents

Introduction by Bill Bryson   vii

Foreword   xix

Introduction   xx

1 The Team   1

2 The Plan   4

3 To the Rankling La   12

4 The Glacier   31

5 Base Camp   47

6 North Wall: the First Assault   57

7 The North Wall Conquered   68

8 Advanced Base to Camp 2   80

9 The Missing Camp   99

10 Higher than Everest   110

11 Higher Still   123

12 Not High Enough   134

13 It Goes!   149

14 Return of the Summit Party   157

15 Farewell to Rum Doodle   167

Introduction

Years ago, in the days before my hair began to leave my head and take up a more sheltered existence in my ears and nostrils, I passed my afternoons and early evenings as a sub-editor on the business section of *The Times*.

It was clean work and the perks included subsidised canteen meals whose principal virtue was that they seemed not to interfere with normal metabolic activity, the right to claim a small monthly cash payment for expenses that were entirely fictitious (though scrupulously and imaginatively recorded on a lengthy docket), and the chance, two or three times a year, to help Philip Howard re-locate his desk by buying some of the many thousands of books that had been submitted to his department for review in the previous few months but had failed to make the cut, often because they were very bad and of no interest to anyone. These Mr Howard sold to a grateful staff at knockdown prices and passed the proceeds on to charity.

Since these sales were generally held between 3 p.m. and 4 p.m., an hour when most of the reporting staff were still only partway through lunch, they were effectively private affairs for the sub-editors. It is not often you see a newspaper sub-editor galvanized, or indeed even in motion, but the announcement of a book sale always had an electrifying effect on the subs' room. In a little over an instant, 60 or more inky-fingered drudges would be thronging Mr Howard's modest sanctum, picking through piles of mostly useless books with an intensity that threatened at times to become unseemly.

It was on one such occasion, as I stood grappling with a thin and obstinate lady from the foreign desk over an anecdotal history of Japanese naval codes or some such thing, that my eye fell on a slender paperback bearing a pen-and-ink sketch of a mountain adventurer lying prone in the snow. The title was *The Ascent of Rum Doodle*.

Sensing a find, I loosed my hold on the lady's bun and claimed the book. Later that evening in the canteen, while dining on Lancashire trotters or some other mysterious dish of Olde England, I cracked open the book and within moments knew that I had found something special.

Perhaps no type of humour is more difficult to sustain over the length of a book than a parody, and I know of none that does it more joyously than *Rum Doodle*. First published in 1956, it is the story of a group of wonderfully endearing incompetents who set out to conquer the world's highest peak, the celebrated but seldom seen Rum Doodle (elev.

$40,000\frac{1}{2}$ feet) in its snowy Himalayan fastness beside the mighty Rankling La.

I just love this book. Everything about it is nearly perfect – the names of the characters, their mannerisms, their sulks and squabbles, their comfortingly predictable haplessness in the face of every challenge. There is Binder, the kindly, dogged, reliably under-insightful leader of the party; Jungle, the route-finder who cannot find his way to any assembly point and is forever cabling apologies from remote and inappropriate locales; Wish, the scientist who passes the sea voyage by testing his equipment and discovers that the ship is 153 feet above sea level; Constant, the language expert who, through errors of grammar and syntax, constantly provokes to fury the 30,000 Yogistani porters; and the terrifying cook Pong, whose arrival at each camp spurs the men on to ever greater heights.

It is all very silly, but hugely enjoyable and brilliantly sustained. I assumed that it was one of those books, like *1066 and All That* or *Diary of a Nobody*, that everyone in Britain was familiar with but that I, as a foreigner, had come to late. The edition I owned contained not a word of information about the author. Wishing to know something of his background, and eager to seek out whatever else he had written, I mentioned the book to friends and asked about it in bookshops, but neither then nor later did I find anyone who was acquainted with either Bowman or his book. For most people, it appears, *Rum Doodle* is the funniest book they have never heard of.

Years passed. My hair began its long descent to various of my cranial cavities and I moved on from *The Times*. *Rum Doodle* went with me when I moved from London to Yorkshire and thence to America, but never did I learn anything more of its author. Then in 1997, after I spoke about the book on a radio programme in London, I received a cheerful and kindly note, written in an elegant hand, from Eva Bowman, widow of the author, and we began to correspond. Eventually, I met her and her son Ghee, and from them I began at last to learn a little more about the long and fitful history of one of my favourite books and the quietly mysterious man who wrote it.

The Ascent of Rum Doodle was published in early 1956 by Max Parrish & Co at a price of 10s 6d. It did not get off to a roaring start. The *Northern Despatch* of Darlington waited almost two years before giving the book a favourable notice. The *Bristol Evening Post* referred to the author as 'W.E. Borman' and, mysteriously, attributed to him an earlier book about airlines. A cherishable reviewer for *Good Housekeeping* admitted that she was some way into the book before realizing 'it is meant to be a farce'. The larger national publications seem almost entirely to have overlooked it. Praise, often lavish, was instead confined to such publications as

The Irish Catholic, The Border Telegraph, The Northern Whig, Western Independent, Kentish Observer, Daily Worker, Bulawayo Gazette and *The Times of India.*

In short, although the book was far from a failure and was translated into several languages, it failed to find a mass audience. In 1957, *Rum Doodle* was followed by *The Cruise of the Talking Fish*, also featuring the heroic Binder in a parody of Thor Heyerdahl's *Kon-Tiki* expedition. This did less well. Soon after, while Bowman was working on a third book in the series, Max Parrish & Co fell into financial difficulties and failed to pay Bowman some of his royalties. Eventually the firm went out of business altogether and Bowman's two comic novels fell out of print.

Meanwhile, unknown to Bowman, *Rum Doodle* had found a devoted following among mountaineers and polar scientists, and the book's mysterious fixations and running jokes had become a topic of active speculation wherever adventurous men gathered. Why, for instance, did the number 153 appear at the heart of so many of the book's jokes? Many grew certain that Bowman had to be a pseudonym for some accomplished and possibly well-known climber. It was widely agreed that no amateur could have created such memorably idiosyncratic characters or written with such easy familiarity about the ardours of climbing without having drawn from real experiences.

In fact, the author was an unassuming structural

engineer from Guildford who had rarely been out of Britain and had never tackled an eminence more lofty than Sca Fell Pike. He had thought up the idea for *Doodle* while walking in the Lakes. It was modelled on a 1937 account of Bill Tilman's Nanda Devi expedition. The number 153 was simply his childhood address.

Specifically it was the number of the house on Borough Road, Middlesbrough, where Bowman and his parents moved soon after his birth in Scarborough in 1911. His early childhood appears to have been a happy one, but when Bowman was 15 his mother died. Two years later his father likewise expired and Bowman and his two younger brothers were permanently separated. The experience cast a shadow over his life that was never entirely dispelled.

After leaving school, Bowman took a job as a draughtsman in an engineering office in Middlesbrough, and developed a passion – necessarily vicarious – for mountaineering, though he became a dedicated fell walker and spent many happy weekends in the Lake District. (He saw real mountains just once, on a trip to Switzerland.) He served in the RAF during the Second World War and from 1947 to 1950 worked for the International Voluntary Service helping to rebuild Germany. In 1950 he joined an engineering firm in London and spent his days designing bridges, power stations and other imposing structures, and filled his evenings by writing.

He married late, in 1958 at the age of 47, and settled with his wife in leafy Surrey, where they had two children. Bowman completed the third book in the Binder series, but it was never published. Nor was anything else he wrote. For the last 25 years of his life, he painted and concentrated on other work – serious and comic poems, a book of short stories, polemics of various types, a treatise on the letter A, and his magnum opus, a reworking of Einstein's theory of relativity.

For years, *Rum Doodle* was either out of print or available only in climbing shops in a facsimile edition published by a Sheffield mountaineering company called Dark Peak. Finally in 1983, almost 30 years after its publication in hardback, Arrow Books issued a paperback edition. This was followed in 1992 by Pimlico with a double edition of *Rum Doodle* and *Talking Fish*. Sales were meagre and, apart from a glowing review in the *Sunday Times*, neither edition attracted much press notice.

In 1981, almost exactly a quarter of a century after *Rum Doodle*'s publication, Bowman discovered to his surprise that in the late 1950s members of the Australian Antarctic Expedition had affectionately attached names from his book to certain geographical features, and that some of these had been incorporated into Antarctic maps. Since 1966, Mount Rumdoodle '(pop. 153, elev. 153)' has been an official designation. Bowman learned of this only because he happened upon a game called The Great Rum Doodle Puzzle, which had been produced by a member of one of the early expeditions. At about the same time, a 250-seat restaurant named Rum Doodle opened in Kathmandu, and is still going strong.

On 1 January 1985, Bill Bowman died at home in Guildford, aged 73. One or two mountaineering journals noted his passing, but no national newspaper ran an obituary.

It is easy to see all this as disappointing, but I prefer not to. It isn't fair, of course, that Bowman didn't enjoy the attention or success his work deserved, but then life often isn't fair. On the other hand, he did have the satisfaction of knowing – as he must have known – that he had written a comic classic. There must equally have been considerable satisfaction in knowing that for all its perennial bad luck and Binder-like setbacks, *The Ascent of Rum Doodle* had achieved a certain immortality. There have always been, will always be, people who adore this book – adore it enough to carry it halfway round the world and even name mountains for it.

And now it is back again. I trust that this is merely the first of 153 printings. In any case, ladies and gentlemen, it is with a sense of pleasure and privilege that I now offer you one of the funniest books you will ever read.

Bill Bryson, 2001

THE ASCENT
OF
RUM DOODLE

To George and Margot

No criticism of any mountaineering
book or method, and no reference to any
mountaineer past or present is intended.

Foreword

by SIR HUGELEY HAVERING, AISC, MPL,

Chairman of the

Rum Doodle Committee

It is with pleasure as well as with a sense of privilege that I associate myself with this account of the climbing of the world's highest mountain. The difficulties were many. They were overcome by the determination of each member of the expedition to give his best to the common cause. No praise is too high for these men. This is a book which should be read – and re-read – by every schoolboy and by all who value human endeavour and fortitude.

Introduction

by O. TOTTER

It is a pleasure and a privilege to associate oneself with this account of the ascent of the world's highest mountain. The obstacles were tremendous. That they were overcome is due to the dogged perseverance, which each member of the team brought to the common cause. It is impossible to praise these men too highly. Every schoolboy should read this book twice, and so should everybody who honours courage and enterprise.

I

The Team

When I was asked by the Rum Doodle committee to lead the assault on the mountain I was deeply conscious of the honour bestowed upon me. To climb Mont Blanc by the Grépon route is one thing; to climb Rum Doodle is, as Totter once said, quite another. I hesitated to accept so great a responsibility, and only the insistence of the committee, particularly of its chairman, Sir Hugeley Havering, persuaded me to change my mind.

I would like at the outset to record my deep appreciation of the selfless devotion and sound judgment with which the Rum Doodle committee – and particularly its chairman – did its job. In no way was that judgment more effective than in the choice of personnel. If I had it all to do over again I would choose those same companions who supported me with such wholehearted and unselfish enthusiasm. I venture to say that no leader has been better served.

Our success was due to two things: magnificent team work and the splendid efforts of the porters, without whom the expedition would have failed.

In advising the committee on the composition of the team I had in mind a principle which has served me well on many occasions: to make one thing fulfil two purposes. Each member of the team was selected to be responsible for a particular organizational or technical job, and each had in addition some special quality which made him valuable as a mountaineer and a companion.

How well this policy succeeded will be evident.

The team members were as follows:

TOM BURLEY, Major in the RASC. In charge of the commissariat. Well known for his prodigious feats of endurance on many mountains, and chosen as our strong man. Had been high. Interrupted a mountaineering furlough in the Alps to join us.

CHRISTOPHER WISH, scientist to the expedition. Excellent on rock. Had been higher than most. Just returned from a successful first ascent in the Andes.

DONALD SHUTE, our photographer. Splendid on ice. Had been as high as most. Lately returned from the Rockies.

HUMPHREY JUNGLE, radio expert and route-finder. Had been nearly as high as most. Recalled from the Caucasus.

LANCELOT CONSTANT, diplomat and linguist. In charge of the porters. Chosen especially for his social tact and good-fellowship. Was expected to go high. Just back from the Atlas mountains.

RIDLEY PRONE, doctor to the expedition and our

oxygen expert. Had been high enough. Barely returned from the Himalayas.

2

The Plan

After three hectic months of preparation we met in London, on the eve of our departure, for a final review of our plans. Only Jungle, who was to have spoken on the use of the radio gear and his own methods of route-finding, was absent. He rang up to say that he had taken the wrong bus and was not quite certain of his whereabouts; but he had just caught sight of the North Star and expected to join us shortly.

Burley, although not at his best – he told me he was suffering from London lassitude – gave us a detailed picture of the transportation arrangements. The object of the expedition was to place two men on the summit of Rum Doodle. This necessitated the establishment of a camp at 39,000 feet stocked with a fortnight's supplies for two, so that in the event of adverse weather conditions the party could wait in comfort for an improvement. The equipment for this camp had to be carried from the railhead at Chaikhosi, a distance of 500 miles. Five porters would be needed for this. Two porters would be needed to carry the food for these five, and another would carry the food for these two.

His food would be carried by a boy. The boy would carry his own food. The first supporting party would be established at 38,000 feet, also with a fortnight's supplies, which necessitated another eight porters and a boy. In all, to transport tents and equipment, food, radio, scientific and photographic gear, personal effects, and so on, 3,000 porters and 375 boys would be required.

At this point the telephone bell rang. It was Jungle, who seemed in the best of spirits. He had, he said, definitely identified his whereabouts as Cockfosters. We congratulated him and said we would expect him shortly.

Burley was congratulated on his masterly command of detail, although Wish expressed the opinion that the weight allowed for scientific equipment was scandalously small. He particularly wanted to take a mechanical glacier shovel and a three-ton pneumatic geologist's hammer, but neither of these indispensable items was allowed for. Burley was quite short with him. He pointed out that shovelling ice on Rum Doodle was quite a different thing from shovelling ice on Mont Blanc, while the rarefied atmosphere obtaining on the mountain would probably render the pneumatic gear impracticable. Wish burst into tears and said that he might as well go home at once, as he did not seem to be appreciated. Constant, in his tactful way, said that he was sure that Burley had no intention of belittling Wish's importance to the

expedition; he had only meant that scientific gear
was out of place on an expedition whose sole
object was to place two men on the summit of
Rum Doodle. This brought in Shute, who said he
very much regretted the implication that scientific
gear was a white elephant; one of the most
important parts of our work would be the investi-
gation of the effects of rarefied atmosphere upon
three-dimensional colour television. Prone, who
was suffering from a severe cold in the head,
muttered something, which nobody quite understood, about 'ibportant bedical baterial' in a kind of
enraged mumble.

Responsive, as a good leader should be, to
human atmosphere, I sensed a hidden discord, and
I quietly reminded all of the words of Totter: Mont
Blanc might be climbed by a disunited party; Rum
Doodle, never. This sobering thought had the
desired effect, helped perhaps by the fact that
Burley, overcome by London lassitude, had fallen
asleep. Wish, who was to share a tent with him,
was much distressed to find that he snored heavily,
but he was consoled by Shute who reminded him
that owing to the attenuation of sound waves in a
rarefied atmosphere the snores would be much less
offensive at high altitudes.

Wish then outlined the scientific programme. In
addition to investigations into the hypographical
and topnological fossiferation of the area he hoped
to collect new data on the effect of biochronical

disastrification of the geneospherical pandiculae on the exegesis of Wharton's warple. He also hoped to bring back a pair of each species of living creature found on the mountain in order to study the possibility of breeding mountaineers capable of living normal lives at high altitudes.

At this point Jungle rang again. It was not Cockfosters, he said, but Richmond. He had seen Cockfosters on a bus, but it turned out that the bus was *going* to Cockfosters. Owing to this he had, of course, set off in the wrong direction, but would be with us shortly.

After this, Shute described the photographic apparatus, the chief of which was a three-dimensional colour cinematographic camera. He hoped to obtain a film record of every aspect of the expedition's work. Suitable love-interest and accident sequences would be added by the company who had supplied the apparatus, and, with a patriotic song incorporated and the original material cut down to a minimum, the film was to be marketed on a world-wide basis as an epic of British heroism. If the summit were reached the successful pair would, if photogenic and under sixty, be offered film contracts for a picture entitled 'Tarzan and the Atrocious Snowmen'.

At this point a telegram was delivered. It read:
SIGHTED BARKING CREEK NINETEEN THIRTY HOURS COURSE WEST NORTH WEST EXPECT SHORTLY

WEATHER COLD BUT FINE JUNGLE. The postmark was Hounslow.

Burley awoke with a complicated gurgle and said that it was all wrong to clutter up a climbing expedition, the object of which was to place two men on the summit of Rum Doodle, with a lot of scientific rubbish. He expressed the opinion that a scientist on an expedition was even more of a nuisance than his gear, which was considerable. He told us about his friend Groag, who shared a tent with a scientist on the 1923 expedition to Tum Teedle. Like all scientists, this one was very absent-minded. One day he inadvertently made tea with copper-sulphate solution instead of water, with the result that he and Groag turned blue and were colour-blind for a fortnight, being unable to distinguish blue from white. One day this scientist stepped off the edge of a snowfield, thinking the blue sky beyond a continuation of the snow. He was saved only by great effort and devotion on the part of Burley, who had the misfortune to be roped to him. Burley said that any ordinary man would have left him to his fate.

Wish said that he did not believe one word of the story. He himself had drunk gallons of copper-sulphate tea with impunity. The blue effect was no doubt due to cardiosynthesis of the bloodstream due to the rarefied atmosphere. He strongly resented the statement that all scientists were absent-minded.

At this point a knock was heard on the door. It was a sergeant from the local police station. A policeman in Lewisham had discovered a furtive stranger loitering near the gas works. He had been found to be in possession of maps and navigating instruments and had been arrested as a spy. He has given his name as Forest and this address as a reference. We gave the necessary assurances and asked the sergeant to transmit a message to the effect that we expected to see Jungle shortly.

Constant then told us about Yogistan, the country through which we must travel to reach the mountain. The natives, he said, were sturdy, independent people, friendly and of imperturbable dignity and cheerfulness. Their language, of which he had made a special study, was a branch of the aneroid-megalithic tongue. It contained no verbs and was spoken entirely from the stomach.

Prone said this was nonsense; if they spoke entirely from their stomachs they would suffer from permanent gastritis. Constant said that this was, in fact, the national disease, being hypodermic in 95% of the population. Prone said that if this was the case he didn't see how they could keep cheerful. Constant said that this was due to their strength of character. He said that he was not used to having his word doubted, and if Prone persisted in his present uncooperative attitude he, Constant, would have to issue an ultimatum.

Prone then spoke to us about the problem of

maintaining the fitness which was so essential to our success. He urged us to follow rigidly the precautions which he had laid down, and handed each of us several pages of closely-typed manuscript. He said that if we followed his advice he could guarantee immunity from illness. Here he broke down with a fit of coughing and had to be thumped on the back. Constant did the thumping, and my impression was that he thumped a good deal harder than was strictly necessary. At any rate, Prone struck back at him, and a nasty incident might have ensued had not Prone been completely overcome by a fit of sneezing which made him quite incapable of defending himself.

I took this opportunity to thank all for their contributions, and remarked that I had no doubt that such little differences of opinion as might appear between us were evidence of the commendable frankness and openness with which we regarded one another, and that I had no reason to suppose that we would not make an efficient and united team. I reminded them of the words of Totter: In an expedition of this kind the desires of the individual must be subordinated to the common cause. Constant said Amen, and on this solemn note we woke Burley and set about making our preparations for the morrow's departure.

★

Next day we sailed from Tilbury. As I stepped aboard two telegrams were handed to me. One read: BEST OF LUCK REMEMBER NOT CLIMBING MONT BLANC TOTTER. The other ran: STRANDED ABERCWMSOSPANFACH WILL FOLLOW BY PLANE SEND HUNDRED POUNDS JUNGLE.

3

To the Rankling La

The voyage was uneventful. My responsibilities as leader prevented me from spending as much time as I should have liked with the others, but I was gratified to see that the *esprit-de-corps* which is so important on expeditions such as ours was uniting our party into a closely-knit community. The importance of the team spirit cannot be overestimated. As Totter once said: When you are swinging helplessly at the end of a hundred-foot rope it is important to know that the man at the other end is a *friend*. It was this spirit, more than any other single factor, which brought success, and I was happy to see it growing during the voyage.

Humour was not lacking. Wish caused much amusement by turning up for dinner one evening with a black eye which he had sustained by walking into a davit, while on the same occasion Burley exhibited a bandaged hand injured during a game of deck tennis. Burley was down most of the voyage with sea lassitude, and it was a surprise to me that he had the energy for tennis. The others kept fit, except for Prone, who alone succumbed to sea-sickness.

Wish was kept busy with his apparatus. He tested our boiling-point thermometers and was able, by averaging the results of many readings, to fix the ship's height as 153 feet above sea level. Burley said this was nonsense, but Wish pointed out that due to the earth's not being a perfect sphere, but larger at the equator than at the poles, the result was quite in accordance with known facts.

Shute took many reels of film, but by an unfortunate oversight he exposed them to daylight, so that no record exists of this portion of the journey.

Constant, to his great delight, discovered a Yogistani family on the lower deck, and spent much time with them improving his knowledge of the language. The association came to a sudden end, however, in a rather strange way. One quiet Sunday afternoon, Constant came running up the stairway in a state of terror, closely followed by a small but powerful oriental person who was waving a knife. After being rescued Constant explained that he had made a trifling error in pronunciation. He had wished to express admiration for the poetry of Yogistan. Unfortunately, the Yogistani word for poetry is identical with the word for wife, except for a sort of gurgle at the end. Being unable, in the enthusiasm of the moment, to produce this gurgle, he had deeply offended his host, with the result we had witnessed.

Constant kept to his own deck for the rest of the voyage.

One day a whale was sighted on the starboard quarter. This was naturally an event of great interest to all, but particularly to myself as it enabled me to make up my mind on the very vital matter of the grouping of the assault party, to which I had given much thought. Our attack on the mountain was to be made by units of two men, who would climb together on the same rope and occupy the same tent. I considered it important that these partners be brought together as soon as possible, to enable them to rub off those rough corners which become irksome at close quarters. I had, however, been unable to reach a decision. Burley and Wish, I had decided long ago, were the ideal combination to fit into a cramped bivouac tent, one being large and the other small; and their personalities and interests were so different that there was little chance of professional jealousy or monotony arising. Shute and Jungle had each shown a lively and controversial interest in the other's special subject, and I thought it would be a pity to part them. Moreover, Shute was a Cambridge man while Jungle had been to Oxford, which would broaden the horizons of both of them. This left Constant and Prone; and I was not at all happy about these two – both having the professional manner, which might prove somewhat stifling in a small tent. But they disagreed so heartily on so many subjects that I began to be reassured, and the incident of the whale put my mind finally at rest. While we were leaning over the rail watching the creature blowing Constant said he wondered whether there was any truth in the Jonah legend. Prone said that he was surprised at such a remark from an educated man, and became so interested in the subsequent discussion that he forgot to be sea-sick. They argued heatedly for the remainder of the voyage and were quite inseparable, which was a great relief to me.

Just before we reached port I received a radio message: UNFORTUNATELY MISDIRECTED BUENOS AIRES SEND FIFTY MILLION PEONS JUNGLE.

★

The rail journey was uneventful. Burley was down with heat lassitude and Prone contracted malaria. Constant remarked that it was a good thing we had a doctor with us. I am sorry to have to record that Prone took exception to this innocent remark and was quite rude to poor Constant, but the latter generously overlooked this as being due to Prone's condition. Constant went into the native portion of the train to improve his knowledge of the language, but soon afterwards a riot broke out and he thought it advisable to retire. He explained that the natives were really friendly people of imperturbable dignity and cheerfulness, but they sometimes allowed themselves to be upset by trifles. We enquired the nature of this particular trifle, but

Constant said it was difficult to explain to a European. Wish spent most of the journey with a stop-watch in his hand timing the telegraph posts in order to calculate the speed of the train. This worked out at 153 miles per hour, but he thought that a certain amount of experimental error should be allowed to cover irregularities in the spacing of the posts. Burley gave him a check and found that the hand of the stop-watch had stuck. This caused much amusement.

★

Our arrival at Chaikhosi was a big event, both for ourselves and for the local people. Constant had arranged that the 3,000 porters should meet the train, so that no time would be lost. As we pulled in we were surprised and gratified to see that a great crowd, which stretched as far as we could see, had assembled to welcome us. When we put our heads out of the window we were greeted by a deafening cheer. Constant remarked on the friendliness of the natives, which, he said, was one of their chief characteristics.

As we stepped off the train we were met by a dignitary whom I assumed to be the local Clang, or headman. Constant engaged him in conversation, putting on his most diplomatic air. They spoke together for several minutes, and a European onlooker might have been forgiven for concluding that they were quarrelling violently; but I told myself that this, no doubt, was the local idiom.

Finally, Constant told us that this was not the Clang at all, but the Bang, or foreman porter, and that the multitude before us were the porters he had ordered.

'If you ask me,' said Prone, 'there are a lot more than three thousand of them.'

I was of the same opinion, but Constant said that nobody had asked Prone and he was sure the number was correct.

'Why not ask your friend?' Prone suggested.

Constant engaged the Bang in another lengthy bout, after which he told us that the man spoke an obscure dialect and did not seem fully conversant with standard Yogistani.

'Let's count 'em, then,' said Prone. 'Line 'em up ten deep.'

Constant turned again to the Bang, and after much noise and gesticulation he explained to us that there was no Yogistani phrase for ten deep and, since military training was unknown in the country, the idea of lining up was not easily conveyed to the Yogistani mind.

I told Constant we would leave him to thrash the matter out with the Bang. He said it was a good idea; we were probably making the poor fellow nervous. As we left they went to it again, holding three fingers in the air and scratching on the dusty ground with sticks.

At the post office a surprise awaited me in the form of a letter from Jungle. He had arrived by plane three days previously and had gone ahead to break the trail.

★

We spent a hungry and uncomfortable night in the station waiting room, for until the dispute with the Bang was settled our equipment could not be unloaded, and in the absence of Constant we dared not risk a night in the local hotel. At daybreak I walked over to the train, to find Constant and the Bang still at it. The former explained to me that the Yogistani word for three was identical with the word for thirty, except for a kind of snort in the middle. It was, of course, impossible to convey this snort by telegram, and the Bang had chosen to interpret the message as ordering 30,000 porters. The 30,000 were making a considerable noise outside, and Constant told me that they were demanding food and a month's pay. He was afraid that if we refused they would loot the train.

There was nothing for it but to meet their demands. The 30,000 were fed — at considerable trouble and expense — and three days later we were able to set off with the chosen 3,000 on our 500-mile journey. The 375 boys who completed our force were recruited on the spot. Boys are in plentiful supply in Yogistan; it appears that their mothers are glad to get rid of them.

★

The journey to the Rum Doodle massif was uneventful. We travelled along a series of river gorges deeply cut between precipitous ridges which rose to heights of 30,000 feet and more. Sometimes we crossed from one valley to another over passes some 20,000 feet above sea level, dropping again to river beds elevated a mere 153 feet or so.

The steepness of the valleys was such that the vegetation ranged from tropical to arctic within the distance of a mile, and our botanists were in their element. I am no naturalist myself, but I tried to show an intelligent interest in the work of the others, encouraging them to come to me with their discoveries. I am indebted to them for what small knowledge I possess in this field.

The lower slopes were gay with Facetia and Persiflage, just then at their best, and the nostrils were continually assailed with the disturbing smell of Rodentia. Nostalgia, which flourishes everywhere but at home, was plentiful, as was the universal Wantonia. Higher up, dark belts of Suspicia and Melancholia gave place to the last grassy slopes below the snow line, where nothing was seen growing but an occasional solitary Excentricular, or old-fashioned Manspride.

The fauna, too, was a constant delight. The scapegoat was, of course, common, as were the platitude and the long-tailed bore. The weak-willed sloth was often met, and sometimes after dark I would catch sight of slinking shadows which Burley identified as the miserable hangdog. One afternoon Shute, in great excitement, pointed out to me a disreputable-looking creature which he said was a shaggy dog. Burley swore that it was not a shaggy dog at all but a hairy disgrace; but this may have been intended for one of his peculiar jokes. Burley's sense of humour is rather weak. He told me one day that he was being followed by a lurking suspicion, which was obviously absurd. But he is a good fellow.

We were naturally all agog to catch sight of the Atrocious Snowman, about whom so much has been written. This creature was first seen by Thudd in 1928 near the summit of Raw Deedle. He describes it as a man-like creature about seven feet tall covered with blue fur and having three ears. It emitted a thin whistle and ran off with incredible rapidity. The next reported encounter took place during the 1931 Bavarian reconnaissance expedition to Hi Hurdle. On this occasion it was seen by three members at a height of 25,000 feet. Their impressions are largely contradictory, but all agree that the thing wore trousers. In 1933 Orgrind and Stretcher found footprints on a snow slope above the Trundling La, and the following year Moodles heard grunts at 30,000 feet. Nothing further was reported until 1946, when Brewbody was fortunate enough to see the creature at close quarters. It was, he said, completely bare of either fur or hair, and resembled a human being of normal stature. It wore a loincloth and was talking to itself in

Rudistani with a strong Birmingham accent. When it caught sight of Brewbody it sprang to the top of a crag and disappeared.

Such was the meagre information gleaned so far, and all were agog to add to it. The most agog among us was Wish, who may have nourished secret dreams of adding the *Eoanthropus Wishi* to mankind's family tree. Wish spent much time above the snow line examining any mark which might prove to be a footprint; but although he heard grunts, whistles, sighs and gurgles, and even, on one occasion, muttering, he found no direct evidence. His enthusiasm weakened appreciably after he had spent a whole rest day tracking footprints for miles across a treacherous mountainside, only to find that he was following a trail laid for him by a porter at Burley's instigation.

★

The porters were unprepossessing. Mountaineering to them was strictly business. An eight-hour day had been agreed on, for which each received *bohees* five ($3\frac{3}{4}$d.). Nothing on earth would persuade them to work longer than this, except money. When not on the march they squatted in groups smoking a villainous tobacco called *stunk*. Their attitude was surly in the extreme; a more desperate-looking crew can hardly be imagined. They were in such contrast to the description which Constant had given us that I was moved to mention the matter to him in a tactful way. He explained that they were used to living above the 20,000-feet line; their good qualities did not begin to appear until this height was reached. He said that they would improve as we got higher, reaching their peak of imperturbable dignity and cheerfulness at 40,000 feet. This was a great relief to me.

Their performance as porters left nothing to be desired. Although short – few were more than five feet in height – they were almost as broad as they were long, and very sturdy. Each carried a load of 1,000 pounds. One cannot praise too highly the work of the porters, without whom the expedition would have been doomed to failure.

The only one of them who was not worth his weight in *bohees* was the cook, whose name was Pong. Of all the barbarous three thousand, Pong was probably the most disreputable and the most startling in appearance. His face had a peculiarly flattened look, as though it had been pressed in by a plane surface while it was still soft. This same flattening seemed to have spread to his soul, for a more morose, unresponsive and uninspiring individual it would be impossible to imagine. His cooking was the reflection of his character. No matter what tempting delicacies he might extract from their tins the final result was an invariable and appalling dark-brown mess which had to be eaten with a strong spoon and contained the most revolting lumps. That we survived his ministrations must be considered a triumph of spirit over matter, for we suffered considerably from indigestion. All attempts to turn him out of the kitchen failed. At the least hint that we were less than delighted with his disgusting concoctions he went into a kind of frenzy and threatened us with knives.

The Bang either could or would do nothing to remove him. Perhaps they had trade union rules about it; however it was, we had to put up with Pong. No small part of our eagerness to get to grips with Rum Doodle was due to the desire, fast becoming an obsession, to get away from him. While on the march I indulged in long daydreams in which Burley and I, in a bivouac tent, cooked delicious repasts, while down below at Base Camp Pong writhed with frustration.

We passed through many villages, the inhabitants of which were invariably sullen and unfriendly, except when Constant made overtures, when they became hostile. He explained that they were not typical of the natives, being a degenerate class who, attracted by the soft living to be made below the 20,000-feet line, had become demoralized and lost their original qualities of dignity and cheerfulness. I may remark here that we came across no sign of habitation above the 20,000-feet line. This, Constant said, was because our course was away from the trade routes.

Shute was anxious to get a good film record of our progress. To do this it was necessary to start ahead of the rest so that he could set up his cameras in readiness for our coming. This simple plan proved more difficult in practice than he had anticipated. On the first three occasions he was unable to assemble his gear before we reached him, and it was as much as he could do to pack hurriedly and catch us up before evening.

Next day he made a specially early start and was not seen again until next morning, when he staggered into camp just as we were making preparations to move off. We had apparently taken different routes. This put him a day behind, for he found it necessary to make up for lost sleep. He did not catch us up until a week later, and then he went ahead and sat up all night to make sure of us. He shot the whole procession as it went past him, and everybody cheered. It was most unfortunate that on this occasion the three-dimensional camera should have developed double vision.

We were daily expecting to overhaul Jungle, although we had seen no trace of the trail which he had gone ahead to break. On the twentieth day we were overtaken by a runner with the following message: 'Captured by bandits. Send *bohees* fifty million ransom. Jungle.'

On the thirtieth day we received the following message by another runner: 'Repeat. Captured by bandits. Send *bohees* fifty million. Jungle.'

We concluded that the first messenger must have decamped with the money. After deep consideration I reasoned that I could place no reliance upon the honesty of these people, and I asked Prone, who was fully recovered from an attack of chicken-pox, to accompany the fellow. On the fortieth day Jungle reached us alone, bringing a ransom demand for *bohees* fifty million for Prone.

It was too much. I decided that the finances of the expedition could stand no more such demands. I therefore sent a trustworthy messenger with the following message: 'Sorry. Bankrupt. Contact Embassy.' On the fiftieth day Prone overtook us. Shortly after being seized by the bandits he had contracted double pneumonia aggravated by whooping cough, and had proved such a nuisance to his captors that they turned him loose. He was a pitiable sight: unshaven, with matted hair and staring eyes. His clothes were torn to ribbons and his boots had no soles. He was suffering from mumps.

Burley, who spent most of the day drowsing in a litter carried by porters, trying to overcome his valley lassitude, awoke one afternoon screaming. He had dreamt that the expedition was starving on Rum Doodle. He produced his calculations and checked them over carefully. It was as he feared. Due no doubt to his attack of London lassitude he had forgotten to allow food for the return journey. Concentrating as he did on the one objective of placing two men on the summit of Rum Doodle, he had forgotten to bring them back again.

I saw that this crisis would tax all my resources as a leader. I said nothing to the others, but carried my burden alone for a week, searching for a way out. At last I was forced to disclose the emergency. Wish gave one look at Burley – and I like to think that even in this crisis one of us, at least, was able to spare a thought for the unhappy author – and commenced to scribble on his thumb nail.

'The solution is quite simple,' he announced. 'Dismiss all but 153 porters and 19·125 boys. The food saved will see us through.'

This was found to be correct. Constant was asked to make the necessary arrangements with the porters. The resulting uproar went on for a week, and Constant was in continual fear for his life. At last we simply could not afford to feed them for another day and were forced to pay them what they demanded, which was too much. The one bright spot was the hope of getting rid of Pong, but for some reason this did not prove practicable. Constant said he sometimes wondered whether the Bang had a vested interest in Pong; but this, I thought, was an unduly cynical view.

★

A month later we stood on the summit of the Rankling La facing the Rum Doodle massif, nature's last citadel against the conquering spirit of man. The great mountain itself, standing majestic against a cloudless sky, struck awe into the hearts of the puny creatures who were soon to set presumptuous foot on those dreadful slopes. What pen could describe our feelings as we viewed the Rum Doodle massif from the summit of the Rankling La?

I will leave the expedition awhile, paused on the summit of the Rankling La facing the Rum Doodle massif, in order to describe the configuration of the mighty mountain and the events which led to our presence on the Rankling La.

The mountain was discovered by allied airmen during the war. Several reports gave heights which varied between 30,000 and 50,000 feet. In 1947 a reconnaissance expedition was sent under Totter with instructions to locate the mountain, ascertain its height and investigate possible routes to the summit. Subsequent expeditions collected more information, but ours was the first serious attempt to climb the mountain.

The Rum Doodle massif is in the shape of a reversed letter M. The summit comprises two peaks: Rum Doodle itself and North Doodle. North Doodle lies to the west of the true summit. The various estimates of the height of the true summit vary considerably, but by taking an average of these figures it is possible to say confidently that the summit of Rum Doodle is 40,000½ feet above sea level.

The main ridge of the massif runs due north and south, broken by the watershed of two rivers, the

Agenda and the Conundra, which divide the ridge into three portions separated by gorges some 20,000 feet deep. The true summit is situated in the centre portion, but North Doodle, although distant from it by little more than a mile, is separated from it by the Conundra gorge. From each summit a ridge runs in a north-easterly direction, the two meeting in a saddle known as the South Col (25,000 feet). The northern face of the South Col descends to the Rankling glacier, which winds around the south-east face of the mountain until it makes a sharp bend to the north-west. From the snout of the glacier emerges the Rankling river, which flows north after crossing the Agenda gorge some three miles below the watershed. The last stroke of the reversed M is completed by the southern ridge of the Rankling valley, which intersects the centre ridge of the massif at a point some two miles west of the true summit.

Our plan was as follows. Base Camp would be established at the head of the glacier at a height of 20,000 feet. Here we would spend some days acclimatizing. During this period reconnaissance would be carried out on the North Wall, which leads to the South Col. Advanced Base would be established on the Col, with an intermediate camp half-way up the Wall. From here to the summit camps would be placed in the most suitable positions. Our tentative plan was to camp at 2,000-feet intervals above Advanced Base, the final camp

– Camp 7 – being at 39,000 feet, only 1,000½ feet below the summit. Each camp would be provisioned for a fortnight, allowing ample safety margin for bad weather.

The great question was: would the mountain go? Totter, in 1947, had written: 'The mountain is difficult – severe, even – but it will go.' Later reconnaissance had questioned whether the North Wall itself would go, but the final verdict had been that it would. Totter himself had summed up the prevailing opinion thus: 'Given team spirit and good porters, the mountain will go.' All the world knows now that it did. It is no small part of my satisfaction that we vindicated Totter's opinion.

But as we stood on the Rankling La we were awed by the mighty bastion which reared its majestic head against the cloudless sky. As we stood there, Constant spoke for all of us:

'She stands like a goddess, defying those who would set sacrilegious feet on her unsullied shrine.'

There was a murmur of agreement. In that moment we were humbled by the magnitude of the task we had set ourselves, and I for one sent up a fervent prayer that I would not be found wanting in the ordeal that lay before us. In such moments a man feels close to himself.

We stood there, close to ourselves, until sunset, the supreme artist, touched the snowfields of that mighty bastion with rose-tinted brushes and the mountain became a vision such as few human eyes have beheld. In silence we turned and made our way through gathering darkness to our halting-place in the valley.

4

The Glacier

Two days later we reached the snout of the glacier and commenced the long haul to Base Camp. Here we roped up for the first time. Jungle went first as route-finder, with Shute, who was to take films of us at some convenient point. With them were ten porters carrying camera and accessories. Burley and Wish followed. The former was suffering from glacier lassitude but was expected to acclimatize shortly. Then came Constant and Prone. The latter had developed German measles but was receiving the best of treatment at his own capable hands. The porters were distributed between the various parties. I stayed behind to meditate for a while on the responsibilities of leadership, and so brought up the rear.

The glacier was over a mile wide, deeply crevassed and littered with innumerable blocks of ice, most of them twenty to thirty feet high. The place was a veritable maze. Even the highest peaks were hidden from sight.

After some hours' march I was gratified to see in front of me the film gear, fully operational, with Shute at the handle. I left him to pack up his things with the help of his porters and carried on. An hour later I was surprised to see him once more, again turning the camera. I concluded that he had passed me without my noticing – as might easily happen – and was glad to congratulate him on his energy. He looked at me in surprise and swore that he had not moved from that spot since setting up his camera over an hour ago. I was about to remind him that this was neither the time nor the place for such witticisms when I was astounded to hear a call from behind. Imagine my amazement when I found that it was Jungle, who, instead of being out in front, had evidently dropped behind and been passed by the rest of us. Following him were a number of porters, in a long straggling line, and then, to our mutual bewilderment, came Burley and Wish.

I must admit that I was completely baffled. It was one of those moments when one doubts one's own sanity. I had, with my own eyes, seen the four people who were now with me set out ahead of me. Of these, I had passed Shute, who had nevertheless appeared ahead of me, while the others, whom I had not passed at all, were now behind me. It was too much to believe that we had passed each other in this complicated way without noticing it.

The question was: where were Constant and Prone?

It was Shute who supplied the answer.

'Jungle, you fool!' he cried. 'You've been and gone round in a circle!'

At once it came clear to me. We were stretched out along the circumference of a circle, everybody following everybody else. Shute had gone on filming us without bothering to identify us as we passed, and we had all gone round twice. If it hadn't been for him, who was the only easily recognizable feature of our route, we might have gone on all day.

Confirmation came shortly afterwards with the arrival of Constant and Prone. I think they must have been suffering from altitude deafness, for they were shouting at each other as though they were half a mile apart instead of only a rope's length. I congratulated myself on my arrangement of the party; two men who could carry on a spirited conversation after several hours' hard marching at 15,000 feet were obviously kindred spirits. It is one of the deeper rewards of leadership to find that one's manipulation of the human element has been successful.

I decided that the occasion was suitable for a halt, and over a glass of champagne we discussed the reasons for the mistake. I asked all to give their opinion candidly, without regard to susceptibilities. It is my belief that men are better friends for facing the truth together, and that evasion of any kind leads to distrust in the long run.

It was encouraging to hear how they responded

to the appeal. Shute was particularly outspoken, and this, I thought, was a good sign in one who was to be Jungle's constant companion.

What none of us could understand was how Jungle, using his compass, as he assured us he had done, could have turned through a circle. The problem was solved by Shute, who made Jungle demonstrate his method. They wandered off together, and soon they, too, were discussing the matter at the top of their voices. Altitude deafness was, I thought, unusually prevalent that day.

When they returned Shute gave us the answer. 'The silly fool forgot to release the catch on his compass,' he told us. 'Naturally, it pointed north whatever direction he took.'

'It might happen to anyone,' I said. It is my experience that a man supplies his best when he is trusted. Nothing saps a man's confidence in himself so much as mistrust from those over him. It would have been fatal to the expedition to allow Jungle to doubt himself – to say nothing of the effect upon him in later life. I take no credit for my forbearance; such things are the essence of leadership; either one has them or one has not.

For this reason I sent Jungle off again after the break, confident that he would not make the same mistake twice.

Nor did he. After we had been on the go for about four hours I found the party at the edge of a vast crevasse – all except Jungle, who was in it. His compass had directed him to it, and rather than make a long detour in a doubtful direction he had insisted on being lowered into the crevasse, intending to climb up the other side by cutting steps. He had been down for two hours and nobody knew whether he was making progress, for his voice was multiplied by echoes and reached the surface as an undecipherable chorus. For all they knew he might be completely stuck.

It is in such moments of crisis that a man's real character is revealed. The veneer of manners and sophistication which enabled him to bluff his way in the civilized world is of no avail to him now. Unless he is heart of oak he will show some crack or blemish, some weakness which will betray him and his comrades. I am glad to be able to record that in this emergency each and all of the party emerged with flying colours. It is perhaps not too much to say that during the final stages of the assault, when things were as black as they could be and only character stood between us and destruction, the confidence engendered by that early incident provided the last ounce of effort which enabled us to win through.

Each, of course, met the crisis in his own way. Burley, with the *sang-froid* of a Napoleon, took the opportunity to recuperate his strength – sapped by glacier lassitude – by taking a nap. Wish was boiling a piece of ice over a primus stove in order to determine the boiling point of ice. Shute had detached the lens of his camera and was correcting it for the reduced refractive index of the rarefied atmosphere. Constant was improving his knowledge of the language by a shouting contest with the Bang. And Prone was treating himself for swollen glands, which he suspected to be incipient.

The behaviour of my companions on this occasion has been, I freely admit it, an example and inspiration to me on more than one occasion when panic threatened. I was both humbled by their calmness and warmed by the confidence which they evidently placed in me, upon whom the responsibility rested. They knew I would not fail them.

But time was pressing. If Jungle was to be rescued from his predicament before nightfall, something had to be done, and done quickly. Obviously, someone must go down after him; but who should it be? Thanks to the morning's incident I had the answer. To Shute alone should go the privilege of risking his life for his friend.

It speaks volumes for Shute's modesty that he did his best to concede the honour to someone else. But I could not allow him to forgo his real desire, and we soon had him dangling on a rope.

After he had descended some distance he disappeared from sight, and his voice became as incoherent as Jungle's. We lowered away until the rope hung slack, then awaited developments.

After some minutes it dawned on me that we

now had two men down the crevasse without being a step further forward. Neither could communicate with us, and we dared not haul on the ropes for fear of injuring them.

The situation was desperate.

It was Burley who, waking up at this juncture, supplied the solution. 'Send down a walkie-talkie,' he said. 'We've carried the blasted things all this way; let's get some good out of them.'

It was a brilliant suggestion. Burley, I decided, must have the honour of descending with a radio set. Like Shute, he modestly declined the privilege, but I insisted. Soon he, too, disappeared from sight. I could have sworn that his last words were something about 'keep my ruddy mouth shut in future'; but this could not have been the case – unless, of course, it was another of Burley's incomprehensible witticisms.

Wish switched on another radio, and we waited breathlessly. Nothing happened. A horrible suspicion came over me.

'Is the set in order?' I asked.

'How the devil do I know?' said Wish. 'Jungle's the expert.'

It was true. None of us knew how to use the radio. Jungle was to have instructed us at the meeting in London, but he had been unavoidably absent.

There was nothing else for it; Wish must go down. He would get Jungle to write down instructions, which would be pulled up by me on a line, one end of which Wish would take down with him.

Down he went; and up, in due course, came the message: 'Batteries not yet installed. Are packed in one of the loads, but Burley does not know which one. Send down champagne.'

This, I decided, would never do. Some channel of communication had to be opened. I scribbled a message: 'Please tell me what to do.' I wrapped this around the neck of a champagne bottle, tied the line round it and lowered it into the crevasse. I gave them five minutes to reply and hauled up the line. The message read: 'Send down another bottle.'

I hope I am not unduly harsh in thinking this an inconsiderate reply; certainly I might be forgiven for thinking so at the time. But, not wishing to appear dictatorial, I did as they requested, sending with the bottle another message: 'I earnestly beg of you to consider my position. All means must be used to extricate you from your predicament. Please advise at earliest convenience.'

Back came the following: 'Yours of even date to hand. Jungle overcome by vertigo. Absolutely imperative you send four bottles of champagne immediately, otherwise cannot answer for consequences.'

This, of course, put the matter in a different light, and I repented my quick judgment. I have since talked the affair over with Totter, who confirms my original opinion that the first message was not quite in the best tradition; but at the time I was anxious to make amends for my unfounded and ungallant suspicion that the request for the second bottle was without justification, and I thereby erred into leniency. That the message was justified must certainly be conceded; we – that is, Totter and I – question only the manner in which it was delivered, which made no acknowledgement of my own difficult position. But it is hard for me, who was at least on *terra firma*, to judge the feelings of those below. Perhaps I have, after all, been unfair to them; if so, I tender sincere apology.

I naturally lost no time in fulfilling the last urgent request, sending with the champagne another appeal for instructions.

The next message read: 'Jungle seized with convulsions. Send down Prone with five bottles.'

This worried me more than I care to say. It seemed to me that champagne was the last thing one would prescribe for convulsions. But Prone, who, sick as he was, pulled himself together manfully when I read the message to him and seemed almost lively for the first time in weeks, assured me that it was just the thing. So we sent him down too.

I gave them time to talk over the situation, then pulled up the cord. Up came an empty bottle, with this message round its neck: 'Bung Ho!'

At the same moment strange sounds began to issue from the crevasse. At first I could not believe my ears, but at last I was forced to the conclusion that my comrades were *singing*. Having some knowledge of British folk-tunes I was able, with some degree of certainty, to identify the music as 'Oh, My Darling Clementine', although, multiplied by echoes, it sounded rather like a full-size choir singing a kind of fugal Clementine. The result was not unpleasing, and I rejoiced that my friends had not lost heart; but unless they intended the song as a code message it was no help to me in my dilemma. I feared that although they were putting up a brave front my companions were in a situation of great peril.

This seemed also to be the opinion of Constant. 'They need me down there!' he said, and before I quite realized what he was about the brave fellow had pushed several bottles into his pockets, belayed the rope to an icicle, and was sliding out of sight.

Time went by, and the singing continued. I raised and lowered the line several times, but no message appeared. I was well-nigh desperate. Six human lives depended on my clear thinking and decisive action; but I was completely at a loss. My impulse was to descend the crevasse myself, even if it were to perish with my colleagues; but this would leave us with no means of communication with the surface.

The porters had long since settled themselves

comfortably on their loads and were smoking the inevitable pipe of *stunk*. I could expect no help from that quarter.

Or so I thought. But I was to receive a lesson on the invaluable qualities of the Yogistani porter, without whom the expedition could not have been successful. The Bang, whose name, by the way, was Bing, suddenly rose to his feet and came across to the crevasse, bringing with him a small but immensely broad and powerful porter, Bung by name. Without a word being spoken, Bung took hold of one end of a rope and was lowered by Bing into the crevasse. Hardly had the rope gone slack when a piercing whistle sounded from below. Bing at once began to haul in again, and you can imagine my astonishment and relief when Bung came safely to the surface holding Burley by his jacket with a mighty fist. Burley, dangling like a puppet, was happily singing 'Yo, Heave-Ho!' – as well he might.

It was too simple. One by one my companions were hauled to the surface, and a cordial reunion took place. I am not ashamed to admit that I shed a quiet tear. Jungle, carried away no doubt by relief at his narrow escape – although I like to think that some small part of his feeling was genuine affection – thumped me so hard on the back that I fell down; and Wish, who seemed a little light-headed after his ordeal, apparently thought it of the greatest urgency that he should inform me that he had measured the depth of the crevasse, which was exactly 153 feet. This seemed to him, for some reason, excruciatingly funny.

When all but Constant had been safely restored to *terra firma* Bing and Bung went back to their comrades. They had evidently forgotten Constant, or were, perhaps, unable to count up to seven. I went over to them and endeavoured to indicate by signs what I wished them to do. I was met by blank scowls. Their meagre intelligence was evidently incapable of grasping my meaning. I lined the rest of the team up, leaving a gap in the middle, and pointed to this gap and to the crevasse, then went through the motions of lowering and raising a rope and greeting a companion saved from the abyss. All nodded encouragingly – a few even applauded – but no one made a move. I went through the whole performance again; this time they took not the slightest notice, but puffed away at their *stunk* as if everything were normal.

The team had clasped each other around the shoulders and, still in line, capered sideways on the ice like a row of chorus girls, singing 'Don't Put Your Daughter On The Stage, Mrs Worthington'. Poor fellows, they were still slightly hysterical from the effects of their ordeal.

I was on the point of unmanly panic when Bing got to his feet, came over to me, leered in a most objectionable fashion into my face and scratched the palm of one hand with the forefinger of the other. He did it in a most deliberate and odious way, as though the act had some esoteric significance.

It was horrible. I honestly thought for a moment that he was trying to bewitch me. One never knows what goes on in the heads of such primitive people. After all, this was the Mysterious East; who knew what might not happen?

The others stopped dancing and gathered round. I appealed to them for advice. What should I do?

It was Burley who told me, although how he came to know about it I cannot imagine.

'Grease it, old boy,' he said; 'grease it.'

I looked at him in astonishment. What was I to grease, and why?

Luckily, Burley took charge. To my amazement he produced a *bohee* ($\frac{3}{4}d.$) and offered it to Bing. The latter shook his head and scratched harder at his palm. Burley added another *bohee*, with the same result.

It seemed to me exactly as if they were bargaining over the price of something. Constant has since explained the matter to me. It appears that the number six is sacred to the Yogistani. Every sixth occurrence of a thing is treated in a special way. The sixth day is a day of rest. The sixth son is put to the priesthood. The sixth pipeful of *stunk* is smoked in honour of one's grandfather; and so on. The prescribed ritual may, however, be waived provided that a suitable offering is made to the gods. In this particular case, five lives had been saved; the gods had been deprived of the presence of five Europeans. To deprive them of a sixth would be the grossest sacrilege, and only a heavy monetary offering could adjust the matter.

The bargaining went on for some time. The Bang was evidently a devout person, for he upheld staunchly the rights of his gods. The final figure was *bohees* a thousand (£3. 2s. 6d.). Payment was made, and the Bang went to the crevasse, taking Bung with him. But this move did not appear to be popular with the rest of the porters, who had been gesticulating and shouting during the bargaining. They now rushed after Bing and Bung and surrounded them; and everybody began to yell at the top of his voice.

The argument went on for some minutes. Evidently, the porters were against the rescue; their superstitious minds were no doubt still uneasy, in spite of the handsome offering.

At last, to our great relief, the Bang appeared to be getting the upper hand. Soon the hubbub was quietened to a mild uproar and the two rescuers forced their way through the mob. In no time at all Constant was restored to us, none the worse for his adventure except for a distressing attack of hiccups. I now realized that it was past time to halt for the night and gave the order to make camp. We turned in a happy and united party.

Some time in the small hours I awoke with a

faint suspicion that there were undercurrents to this episode. Why, for instance, had the dramatic rescue taken place only when it was too late for further marching? I put away such ignoble thoughts at once, and mention them only as evidence of the deterioration which sets in at high altitudes due to the rarefied atmosphere.

★

Next morning no one was fit to travel. Burley, in reaction from his magnificent effort of the day before, had gone down again with glacier lassitude, and Prone was prostrate with a sharp attack of pins and needles. The others complained of glacier depression and pressed Prone to prescribe champagne. But the latter was, unfortunately, too ill to attend them, and I dared not on my own initiative take the responsibility of administering so potent a medicine.

I need hardly say that champagne was carried for medicinal purposes only.

I was anxious to push on to Base Camp. We were already behind in our programme. Moreover, we were still on the glacier, and at any moment a crevasse might open beneath our feet, precipitating us into the abyss. I therefore gave the order to strike camp.

My companions were hoisted on to the backs of stalwart porters, and even I, feeling somewhat overcome by recent emotional experiences, allowed myself to be transported in the same way.

Bing, the Bang, who had shown initiative in the crevasse incident, was sent ahead as route-finder. The day passed without incident. I awoke at noon to find the vast precipice of the North Wall towering above us. We were at Base Camp.

5

Base Camp

At Base Camp we set about the task of preparing ourselves for the job ahead. Our first concern was to acclimatize. The problem of getting the best out of the members of such an expedition is always one of the most difficult which a conscientious leader must face. It is three-fold, and may be discussed under the headings: fatigue, acclimatization and illness. The question of fatigue is two-fold: if a man is overworked he becomes tired; if he is underworked he becomes lazy. The question of acclimatization is three-fold: first, a man must spend some time high before he is able to work effectively. Second, if he stays high too long he deteriorates. The effect of being high is thus very similar to that of being in a sleeping-bag. Third, if he goes low he will probably be able to recuperate. The whole thing is complicated by the psychological factor; and on this score I have but one rule: a contented climber is a good climber.

Thanks to the splendid work of Prone the expedition was remarkably free from illness. All were fit and well, except poor Burley, who had

fallen victim to Base Camp lassitude and consequently was not acclimatizing as quickly as the
others, and Prone, who was smitten with mysterious and complicated symptoms, namely: pallor,
profuse sweating, pulse rapid and soft, temperature
sub-normal, deep breathing and sighing, restless-
ness and thirst, cold extremities, faintness, dizziness
and buzzing in the ears. Poor fellow, he was much
distressed, both by his condition and by the fact
that he was unable to diagnose his ailment. The
problem was finally solved by Constant, who
produced a first-aid manual and pointed out that
the symptoms were exactly those of haemorrhage,
except that the last two were missing, namely:
insensibility and death. He said there was still hope.
Prone then discovered that he had cut himself in
the ear while shaving and was slowly bleeding to
death. After stopping the bleeding by holding ice
against his ear and afterwards treating himself for
surgical shock and a frostbitten ear, he went down
with Italian measles.

The days of acclimatization were spent accord-
ing to the character and duties of the individual.
Burley superintended, as well as his condition
would allow, the unpacking and repacking of the
stores and, in his more active moments, evading
the scientific attentions of Wish, who insisted on
subjecting him, as the heaviest man of the party, to
a harrowing process known as a fatigue test.

Wish was fully occupied with research of various

kinds. At almost any time of day he could be seen shovelling or drilling the ice of the glacier, taking thermometer readings at various strategic points, hitting rocky outcrops with hammers, or calibrating his boiling-point thermometers. He offered a prize of $1\frac{1}{2}$d. for every specimen of creature brought to him, and 3d. for every Wharton's warple; but although we spent much time poking into crevasses and lifting stones none of us was able to supplement his income. Wish chose me, the lightest of the party, as his second subject for the fatigue test. Being anxious to encourage every aspect of the expedition I did my best to satisfy his demands, but I became so exhausted that I had little energy to spare for the others, which was rather unfair; but no complaints were heard, which was a tribute to the prevailing team spirit.

Shute took the opportunity to give his gear a thorough try-out. His favourite test-piece was myself running up and down the hill which Wish had chosen for his fatigue test. I could only hope that these sequences would not be given, in the final film, the emphasis which they received at the time.

Jungle's job was to prepare the walkie-talkie apparatus and to instruct us in its use. I have always had a horror of electrical gadgets and I was relieved to find that our sets were quite simple to operate, besides being too weak to hurt us. But although the gear was simple the method of using it was not.

In my ignorance I thought that we would call each other up as one does on the telephone. But it is much more complicated than that. In the first place, you never address a person by his real name. Code names are used. Jungle gave us our code names, which were as follows:

BURLEY: Deadweight	CONSTANT: Applecart
WISH: Fiddler	PRONE: Ailing
SHUTE: Dickie-bird	MYSELF: Binder

There was some argument about Jungle's code name. He himself had picked 'Pathfinder', but this, for some reason, proved unpopular with the others. Shute, rather tactlessly I thought, suggested that 'Pathloser' would be more appropriate. Eventually we compromised with 'Wanderer', but Jungle seemed hurt.

Then we had to learn the language. One must never, under any circumstances, speak in the normal manner. To say, for instance, 'yes', 'no' or 'very well' is quite unheard of. Instead, one must use such expressions as 'that is correct', 'can do', 'will do', 'Roger', and so on. Two o'clock becomes 'fourteen hundred hours' and midnight, for some obscure mathematical reason, must never be referred to. To go East is to 'proceed zero-niner-zero', and 20,000 feet becomes 'angels twenty'.

There was also an elaborate ceremonial to be observed when calling up and replying. Finally, we were forbidden to use our ordinary voices; we must speak in a kind of chant which would make it difficult to tell one voice from another.

The younger members seemed to get a good deal of innocent fun from this ritual, but I must confess that I found it a little confusing.

The radio sets were made small to save weight, and their range was limited. It might sometimes be necessary to have messages relayed via one or two intermediaries. In view of certain youthful experiences at children's parties I decided that some practice was advisable. I asked the party to form a large circle over the whole width of the glacier, so that messages could be sent right round. At first I was quite unable to think of a message. My brain seemed to have frozen, and I stood for some minutes feeling foolish. At last, I managed somehow to compose the first message: 'How serene is Rum Doodle in the morning light.'

This came back as 'Binder's butter beans.'

After some thought I sent out the following: 'Please pay very careful attention to the message.' This, too, came back as 'Binder's butter beans.'

This was absurd. As an experiment I sent out: 'Binder's butter beans.' This returned as: 'The voice of the leader is sweet music in the ears of the followers.'

This sort of thing went on all morning. I was determined not to give up until we had mastered the technique, and greatly to my delight the messages began coming through perfectly, without any apparent reason for the change, just before lunch time.

By great coincidence we had butter beans for lunch, which I thought rather amusing.

Some of us were inclined to be sceptical about the value of the radio; but we were shortly to receive striking proof of its usefulness. I was taking a walk one morning by myself, in order to meditate on the responsibilities of leadership, when my walkie-talkie began to buzz. I put it to my ear and heard a voice:

'Applecart to Binder. Applecart to Binder. Are you receiving me? Over.'

I flicked the switch to 'transmit' and said: 'Binder to Applecart. Binder to Applecart. Receiving you loud and clear. Are you receiving me? Over.'

Back came the reply: 'Applecart to Binder. Receiving you strength eight. Turn up two notches. Over.'

I turned up two notches and said: 'Binder to Applecart. Have turned up two notches. Are you receiving me? Over.'

'Applecart to Binder. Receiving you loud and clear. Good-morning. Do you know where cork-screw is? Over.'

'Binder to Applecart. Please say again. Over.'

'Applecart to Binder. I say again. Receiving you

loud and clear. Good-morning. Do you know where corkscrew is? Over.'

'Binder to Applecart. Good-morning. Corkscrew is in right-hand pocket of spare trousers. Over.'

'Applecart to Binder. Roger. Over and out.'

One wonders how earlier expeditions managed at all without the boon of radio.

★

Constant had the job of paying off the redundant porters and instructing the remainder in their future duties. We retained 88 porters and 11 boys for the return journey, the rest being dismissed. Of the 99, those who were not actively employed on the mountain were to move Base Camp to another position where it would be safe from avalanches. Constant considered that they could be left to do the job themselves, as he had made everything quite clear to them. This was a relief to me, as every available European would be needed on the mountain.

★

I have made a special study of the effects of rarefied atmosphere on human behaviour, and had asked the others to tell me of any unusual experiences which might occur to them on the mountain. Even at the comparatively moderate height of Base Camp altitude effects were already perceptible. During an impromptu game of cricket Burley swore at the umpire – a thing which could never happen at sea level – while Wish showed a tendency to take more than his share of marmalade. But these were temporary effects which would disappear with acclimatization.

It was interesting to notice how the diverse characters of my companions influenced their choice of literature. Burley whiled away his hours of lassitude with *Bulldog Drummond*. Wish could be found almost any evening huddled over a melting block of ice reading *Martians and Atom Men*. Shute relaxed with *Three-Dimensional Murder*. Jungle displayed an unexpectedly romantic soul with *Love in the Labyrinth*, while Prone was never to be seen without a copy of his own work *The Secret of Radiant Health*, except when he had mislaid it.

My duties did not allow of frivolous relaxation. But it is worth recording that Bing, the Bang, spent much of his leisure immersed in a Yogistani translation of *Three Men in a Boat*.

We foregathered in the evening for a social hour, and many a spirited discussion took place at these gatherings. On one occasion we discussed the old question: should oxygen and other artificial aids be used on mountains. Burley said that it was a lot of ruddy lumber; more trouble than it was worth. He told us about his friend Baffles, who carried an oxygen set weighing forty pounds to the summit of Mi Wurdle, only to find when he got there that the apparatus had been out of order all the time. Wish said that this remark was typical of the layman's ignorant point of view. We had a unique opportunity to test our gear under rigorous conditions, and our duty was to do so. He asked Burley why, if he disagreed with its use, he was willing to use it. Burley asked whether Wish expected him to climb the ruddy mountain naked. Wish said that this was a typically unscientific argument. He said he had long been aware that to some the ascent of the mountain partook of the frivolous nature of a sporting event. He himself took a sterner view. To him, the climax of our efforts would be the fulfilment of his own self-dedicated task of determining the melting-point of ice on the summit. He reminded Burley that without oxygen the exacting intellectual efforts which this delicate experiment demanded would be quite impossible. Burley, rather tactlessly I thought, said that, speaking with wide experience and an excellent memory, he could recall nothing which approached this for futility. He said that nobody except a demented scientist would want to melt ice on the tops of mountains, and even if he did, who cared what the temperature was? He told us about his friend Strokes, who had had the ice melted under his feet by a scientist on the summit of the Schmutzigstein and had lost three toes in consequence. He said that any scientist was a menace on a mountain.

While they were arguing this point with their usual commendable frankness Shute said that without artificial aids the taking of three-dimensional films would also be impossible; and this prompted Jungle to remark that that was sufficient justification for doing without them. His own motive in climbing was to escape from mechanical civilization and everything that it stood for, especially films. Constant said that he deplored the narrow outlook of the others. *He* climbed solely to demonstrate the triumph of the spirit over adverse circumstances. He said that artificial aids were unsportsmanlike; if they were carried to their logical extreme we might find climbers impaling the summit of a mountain with a long-range harpoon attached to a rope ladder. If summits could not be climbed unaided they were better left unclimbed. Prone said this was rubbish; if artificial aids were refused tents and clothing must go with them. He asked Constant if his triumphant spirit was prepared to climb Rum Doodle in a loincloth, or worse.

Although I believe in plain speaking between friends I really felt that it was being overdone on this occasion. I therefore reminded all of the words of Totter on the subject: No practical mountaineer would refuse the help of science, but there are limits. I expected this to put an end to the discussion – for what more is there to say? – but nobody seemed to take any notice. It was obvious to me that we were still suffering from the rarefied atmosphere.

6

North Wall: the First Assault

At last, all were considered acclimatized, with the exception of Prone, who had developed blood-pressure; and we set out to assault the North Wall. I sent off the following message by runner: 'Moving to attack North Wall, the tremendous precipice which rears above us 5,000 feet against the sky. The question on all lips is: "Will it go?" and every heart whispers a confident: "Yes, it will!" The spirit of the team is excellent and the porters are beyond praise. All in good health.'

The North Wall is a sheer glass-like face of ice broken only by rock, snowfields, ice-pinnacles, crevasses, *bergschrunds*, ridges, gulleys, scree, chimneys, cracks, slabs, *gendarmes*, *Dames Anglaises*, needles, strata, gneiss and gabbro. A formidable obstacle, and one to daunt the hearts of a disunited party supported by mediocre porters. Our plan was to establish Advanced Base on the South Col, which is immediately above the North Wall; but it was expected that one intermediate camp would be needed.

We had already reconnoitred the lower slopes of the Wall, and two schools of thought had arisen concerning the best method of tackling it. Wish, our cragsman, favoured the direct ascent of a precipitous rock-face which led to what seemed easy going higher up. Shute, the ice expert, preferred a steep slope of ice which likewise appeared to ease off towards its upper extremity. Since no final decision was possible it had been decided to try both ways simultaneously. Shute and Jungle would tackle the ice, Wish and Burley would attack the rock. Constant and I, after tidying up at Base, would follow on to support either party.

Constant and I moved off shortly after midday, and we had not yet left the glacier when my radio buzzed. It was Jungle in a high state of excitement. Shute was stuck half-way up his ice-field, having lost his ice-axe and being afraid to come down. Jungle's own axe was sunk in the ice with the rope belayed to it. He dared not remove it in case Shute should fall. Would we please come and help him?

This was alarming news. I immediately assured Jungle that we would be with him as quickly as possible, and we set off at full speed. But we had gone no more than a few paces when Constant disappeared into a crevasse. The rope tightened between us and I was jerked on to my face. In the excitement I let go of my ice-axe and found myself being pulled towards the lip of the crevasse with no means of stopping myself. I was within two yards of the edge when I stopped. The rope had cut into the ice and the increased friction had saved me.

But it was a desperate situation. When I tried to rise the rope pulled me forward as Constant fell still further. Only by lying spreadeagled could I get sufficient friction to halt his fall. I could do nothing to save Constant; unless help came there was no hope for us.

Our only chance was the radio. With my heart in my mouth I edged my right hand nearer and nearer, and at last I was able to place the apparatus near my face. I called up Burley and Wish. The former replied, and I asked him to hurry to our help.

To my consternation he informed me that they, too, were in difficulties. Wish was stuck half-way up his rock-face, being unable to move up or down. Burley was completely exhausted; evidently he had not fully acclimatized. He had himself been on the point of calling for help.

There was only one solution. Jungle must leave Shute, who at least was belayed to Jungle's ice-axe, and come to our help. The three of us would then rescue the others. Jungle acknowledged his instructions and told us he was setting off.

I hope I never have to endure such an ordeal again. Every minute was an hour, every hour an eternity. A hasty move on my part might send both Constant and myself crashing into the abyss. My nose itched, but I dared not scratch it; it froze, but I dared not rub it. I was getting colder and colder. Constant, with whom I could converse in shouts, was in a similar predicament. He was unhurt, but as cold and miserable as I was, if not more so.

After a long time the radio buzzed. It was Jungle. He had lost his way.

My heart sank, and Burley, who was listening in, gave a groan. It was surely all up with us now. I was suddenly seized with an overwhelming sense of the pathos of it all. We, who had set off so confidently, who had worked so hard and come so far; we who were our country's hope and a world's heroes: we were to perish miserably in this stern country, far from home and dear ones.

It was so sad that I could not hold back the tears. The tears froze immediately and I found myself stuck to the glacier by two icicles and in an even worse state than before.

I told Constant the news and did my best to comfort him. Poor fellow, he took it well, and so did Burley when I spoke to him. If we were to die, at least we would die like gentlemen.

There was still hope that Jungle would find us, but so low was I that I put little trust in him.

The day wore on.

I was, I think, half unconscious when an idea came to me. The porters! They had saved us before; could they save us again?

The only way of communicating with them was via Prone. None of the porters would touch the radio; I think they thought it was witchcraft. The question was: was Prone within hearing of a radio, was the radio operational, and was he in fit condition to answer it?

I called and waited, called and waited again; and went on calling. I became frantic with anxiety.

Then I realized that I was doing it wrong. I stopped buzzing and spoke into the microphone:

'Binder to Ailing. Binder to Ailing. Are you receiving me? Over.'

And then came the words that will ring in my ears to my dying day.

'Ailing to Binder. Ailing to Binder. Receiving you loud and clear. Are you receiving me? Over.'

I could have wept – had not the icicles been a reminder of the folly of doing so. I explained the situation to Prone and asked him to get the Bang. He did so, and I began the difficult business of instructing him. Constant translated my messages into Yogistani and I passed them on as accurately as I could to Prone, who gave them at third hand to Bing.

It was hopeless. My stomach and Prone's were quite unused to pronouncing Yogistani. The noises we produced would have been a disgrace in any company; as vehicles of communication they were a total failure. Constant said that the replies which I passed on to him bore no relation at all to the problem under consideration. They would, he said, if uttered in the streets of Chaikhosi, result in imprisonment for life, if not worse. They were, he imagined, without precedent or parallel in the whole history of spoken language. He himself had never imagined that such statements were possible; if he ever came out of the crevasse alive he would have to reconsider his whole philosophy in the light of what I had said. He begged me to keep my stomach closed and tell Prone to do the same. If the least suspicion of what he had heard should reach the ears of the Bang, the result might well be a massacre; at the very least, the porters would desert, or would be incapacitated for further work.

This was serious. There remained one hope: was Prone fit to travel?

No, he said; it was out of the question. His legs would not support him.

But he could be carried? Yes; he was fit enough for that.

And so it was arranged. Again, we waited, but this time in high hope. Prone, carried by the Bang, gave us a running commentary on his progress.

Then they were with us: Bing, short and immensely powerful, with Prone pick-a-back; Bung, shorter still but equally sturdy; and a third porter, Bo by name, who was even shorter and sturdier.

In no time my icicles were hacked away and Constant hauled to the surface, chilled but otherwise none the worse. Bing and Bung were despatched to the rescue of the others, while

Constant and I staggered back to Base Camp accompanied by Bo with Prone on his back.

The others returned within the hour. Bing had climbed up to Shute and brought him down under his arm, and later had done the same for Wish. Both were shaken by their ordeal and had to be treated with champagne. Burley, who had been carried back, went to bed with a bottle.

The question now was: where was Jungle? We called him by radio but failed to make contact. Shute said that we had probably seen the last of him; he would turn up next year in Vladivostock, or the year after that in Valparaiso, and write a book entitled *Route-finding in Asia and America*. He said that since Jungle was aiming for Base Camp it was a mathematical certainty that he would never reach it; we had better forget about him.

I could only conclude that Shute was still suffering from shock.

A search party was clearly the thing. But none of us was fit to go out again. Could the porters help us? Constant put it to the Bang. The latter immediately called out the porters and made them form a straight line with one end at the camp and the other far out on the glacier. With the camp as centre they described a circle, and it was not long before Jungle was caught and restored to us, tired but sound. He was quite surprised to find that we had been anxious about him and inclined to take it as a reflection on his competence. I told him that he must allow for our natural over-anxiety at the bare possibility of losing him. He saw my point, and seemed satisfied.

★

Next day we held a council of war. The North Wall was proving a tougher proposition than we had anticipated; our plans would have to be drastically revised. Moreover, Burley said that he would not in any circumstances allow himself to be alone on a rope again with Wish. he had, he said, promised his fiancée that he would take no unnecessary risks, and cragsmen who became cragbound at the very earliest opportunity were clearly an unnecessary risk. He said that his frequently-expressed opinion of the nuisance value of scientists upon mountains had been fully vindicated. A mountaineer scientist was, he said, one of the worst and most dangerous types of split personality, and not to be relied upon except to do the wrong thing.

Wish retorted that the leading man on a rope had the right to expect help from the second. If Burley had been half a mountaineer, instead of wholly a handicap, yesterday's unfortunate incident would never have occurred. He said that big men were notoriously clumsy on crags, and it would suit *him* very well indeed if Burley stayed at the bottom of the mountain, where he could do the least amount of damage. Those of us who had fiancées, he said, owed it to them to keep as far away from Burley as possible.

Jungle broke in now, saying that he himself had no fiancée, but if he had he would consider it his elementary duty to keep away from Shute, who, he said, was as little to be trusted with an ice-axe as a Red Indian on the warpath. Shute, considerably agitated I thought, said that *his* fiancée had expressly warned him against passengers who let other people do all the work and got lost when their turn came. He said that the sight of Jungle on the other end of one's rope was enough to make the safest iceman drop his axe. He said that nothing would induce him to venture out alone with Jungle again.

All this was somewhat bewildering. It was quite clear, of course, that my companions had not yet recovered from their recent shaking-up. That portion of their remarks which was not friendly plain speaking was doubtless due to nervous reaction from their ordeal; in a day or two they would be their normal hearty selves again. In the meantime I had the responsibility of nursing two friendships, and this did not promise to be easy. My mind was further confused by trying to decide who had a fiancée and who had not.

In the end, all I could think of was to remind them again that Rum Doodle was not Mont Blanc. Shute said that he was glad to be reminded of this, as he had completely forgotten the fact. He asked me if I could recall any of Totter's remarks on the subject which might be of help to him in future. I quoted to him Totter's famous remark: To climb Mont Blanc is one thing; to climb Rum Doodle is quite another. Shute thanked me and said that this was one of the soundest things he had ever heard; it would, he said, be a great inspiration to him. He would be quite conscious in future that he was not on Mont Blanc, and would behave accordingly. He said that had he been on Mont Blanc he would have been delighted to have Jungle as his partner; as, however, he was not on Mont Blanc, but on Rum Doodle, he insisted on having a third person on the rope – preferably a porter.

This seemed reasonable enough. Yesterday's lesson was that two on a rope were ill-fitted to cope with an emergency. A porter with each pair would greatly increase our factor of safety. But since the bivouac tents were made to accommodate two, it would have to be four on a rope: two Europeans and two porters. This arrangement would have the additional advantage that the porters would be able to carry complete equipment for all four, so that each rope would be a self-contained unit capable of looking after itself, if necessary, for several days.

Burley pointed out that this would upset all our planning; but since it would mean that he would no longer have Wish all to himself he was heartily in favour of it. The others were just as enthusiastic, and we decided to adopt the idea. I was greatly pleased by our unanimity, which seemed to me to reflect the spirit of the expedition.

7

The North Wall Conquered

On the following day we set off once more. Burley was too weak to leave his sleeping-bag so I sent Shute and Constant away together with their two porters, followed by Wish and Jungle with theirs. Before setting off myself I sent a runner with a despatch: 'Reorganizing for second assault on North Wall. All fit and well. Team spirit beyond praise and the porters are excellent.'

That day's work was truly phenomenal. On arriving at the foot of his ice slope Shute wisely decided to give his porters lessons in icecraft. He first showed them how to cut steps, then let them try it for themselves. They picked it up very quickly – so quickly, in fact, that Shute and Constant could hardly keep up with them. They mounted the steep slope as rapidly as they were able to climb in the rarefied atmosphere. Both said they had never seen anything like it. The porters showed no sign of tiring; they kept on and on, in spite of their full loads and the work of chipping steps in hard ice.

When Wish and Jungle arrived at the ice wall the first party were nearly out of sight. It would obviously have been foolish to ignore so satisfactory a staircase, and they abandoned the idea of tackling the rock-face again.

I arrived some hours later. By this time neither party was to be seen. I called Wish on the radio. He told me what had happened. He said that all the Europeans were on the verge of exhaustion due to the pace set by the porters. They would certainly reach the South Col. He advised me to go back to Base Camp and follow next day with all the equipment needed at Advanced Base. He particularly asked me not to forget the medical equipment, which was likely to be of more use there than at Lower Base.

So back I went to Base Camp, not sorry to have a chance to rest and to spend some friendly hours with Burley. My affection for this forthright giant had been growing ever since our first meeting. A leader should not have favourites, but I must confess that from all my companions I would have chosen Burley to share a tent with.

I found him in his sleeping-bag and said that I proposed to spend the night with him. He said it was kind of me, but he really thought that Prone needed me more than he did. Prone, he said, would be left quite alone at Base and would be happier during his lonely vigil if he had the memory of one night of companionship. This was very unselfish of him and, disappointed though I was, I could not but see that my duty was with the lonely one.

I found him in his sleeping-bag. He also was grateful but unselfish, saying that he would not dream of depriving Burley of my company. I told him I would not hear of such a sacrifice, and soon we were settled in for the night.

Poor Prone seemed quite low, and to brighten him up I encouraged him to talk about his home. Had he a fiancée? I asked. He said no, his wife was the unsympathetic kind and his children considered one mother quite enough.

I apologized for my blunder, but said I was surprised to hear that he was married; Sir Hugeley had told me that he was a bachelor. Prone said that Sir Hugeley was welcome to his opinion on this, as on every other subject; but his own impression was different. I said that I supposed he found family life congenial. He said, on the contrary, he found it unsupportable.

I urged him to tell me more, saying that a trouble shared was a trouble halved. The poor fellow was reluctant at first, but I overcame his shyness and he told me his sad story. He was of poor family. His father was an unemployed oil-stroker of the old-fashioned sort with a strong pride in his craft and a horror of receiving charity. To send his son to medical college he forced himself to swallow his pride. Prone said that the daily sight of his father swallowing his pride had been the strongest impression of his early manhood. Not only did his father swallow his pride, he wore it to the bone for the sake of his son, drawing benefit from six different charities under eight different names, writing begging, threatening and anonymous letters, picking pockets, robbing mail-vans and women's handbags, burgling houses, taking toffee from children and writing penitent articles for revivalist journalists. Such willing and grinding sacrifice had inspired the young Prone to dedicate himself to the fulfilment of his father's desire. He resolved that no obstacle should prevent him from attaining the distant goal of GP.

After many years of devoted study his ambition was achieved. To provide the money for his purchase of a practice his father made the final sacrifice, accepting the honorary treasurership of a charitable organization which offered unlimited scope for embezzlement. Prone became a practising doctor.

His very first patient was a widow suffering from acute horror and malevolence due to reading her small son's comics. She hated the young doctor at first sight and made up her horrible mind to marry him. She told him that unless he took her to wife she would accuse him publicly of having mislaid her medical card. Rather than risk disgrace and the shattering of his father's dreams, Prone consented. They were married at Gravesend on Hallowe'en.

His married life had been a long martyrdom. His

wife, he said, was a fiend in human shape. A gracious lady to the outside world, she was a devil to him. The things she did were too horrible to be mentioned. Their children, who numbered eight and one to come, were fitting offspring of such a monster, each more loathsome than the last – the one to come being, by a process of extrapolation, truly ghastly in his imagination. Nobody, said Prone, could possibly have the faintest idea of what he had gone through. His Saturday afternoons were nightmares.

I was deeply grieved by this pathetic story. I told Prone that he had my full sympathy and offered my help in any way which might be of use to him. He said that it was very kind of me; as a matter of fact there was one little thing I could do: he wished to test an anti-pester serum; did I mind if he tried it on me?

Naturally I was glad, both at his change of mood and of my chance to be of use to him. He got out his hypodermic syringe and gave me a large injection.

He told me afterwards that he was quite satisfied with the result. The effect was to send me to sleep at once; and so ended the only heart-to-heart talk which I was able to have with Prone.

★

Next morning I rose late, feeling for some reason quite below par. I had the task of organizing the porters in Constant's absence without understanding a word of their language. Luckily, the equipment was already prepared; all I had to do was to get hold of the porters one by one and lead them to their loads. It turned out, however, that they had their own ideas as to who was to carry what, and a good deal of confusion resulted. We were just ready by lunch time, when, of course, they all went off to eat. After lunch it all had to be gone through again, and it was quite late when we were at last ready to move off.

I had difficulty in persuading Prone to allow the medical equipment out of his hands, but he finally agreed to let me take it, after taking out anything which he himself might need. We had a long discussion about whether the champagne – which, of course, was part of the medical equipment – should be taken to the South Col. We compromised by leaving one case behind; he needed it particularly, he said, as he was about to contract anaemia.

Burley was unable to give me any help, being still sleeping-bag-ridden. But he appeared, good fellow that he is, to see me depart. He was disturbed when he saw that I had the medical equipment; he had not realized that it was going to the South Col.

We set off, after I had taken an affectionate farewell of Prone, and had gone only a little way when Burley overtook us. He did not like, he said, to see me going off alone, and as he was suddenly feeling much better he had decided to accompany me. He would, he said, be able to acclimatize more quickly on the Col.

I was both impressed by his fortitude and touched by his consideration. It may have been due to his kindness that I felt homesick that morning. I told Burley about my family and friends and showed him some photographs when we halted. The dear fellow was quite gruff – one might almost have said rude. He, too, was evidently feeling the pull of home and found it difficult to hide his feelings. I put a friendly hand on his shoulder, and he gave a little snort. That snort told me more than words could have expressed. I suspected that his decision to accompany me had been wrung out of him by a desire for my companionship, and that he wished to say something to me but could not find the words. So I said to him, kindly: 'Is there anything you want to tell me, old chap?' He said: 'Don't be a bloody fool!' which, I thought, was eloquent of the dear fellow's state of mind.

The rest of the day was a trudge up steps already cut in the steep ice. Fixed ropes had been put in the more difficult places, and we had little to do but mount steadily, maintaining the rhythm which is so necessary to high-altitude climbing. In spite of their heavy loads the porters showed no tendency to fall behind; they were doing splendidly.

In the late afternoon we strode up the last gentle slope to Advanced Base. There was no sign of life, but as we drew near the sound of loud snores from the four tents told us that our companions and their porters were recuperating after their strenuous efforts of the previous day.

We lost no time in pitching our tents, and soon Pong was busy over the pressure stoves. How he came to be at Advanced Base I was unable to decide; certainly I had had no intention of bringing him with me. I wondered, in one moment of ungallant suspicion, whether Prone had pushed him on to the end of our procession. It would have been an unBritish thing to do; but the temptation would be great, and a sick man might well be forgiven for yielding to it. I must say, in fairness to Prone, that he repudiates any such action. His theory is that Pong came along of his own initiative, being furious at the thought of losing so many victims.

Be that as it may, the others, when they emerged from their tents at the cry of 'Come and get it!' were, in their turn, furious when they recognized the familiar handiwork, and I am obliged to record that hard words were said. My plea of innocence was met by a counter-charge of incompetence, and dinner, besides being, as usual, the day's worst ordeal, was also the occasion of acrimony.

It was clear to me that we were not yet acclimatized; and this was confirmed by the others.

They had, they said, been completely worn out by the hard pace set by the porters in their step-cutting. They advised great caution in the employment of porters for this purpose; their brute strength and endurance was to be reckoned as one of the natural hazards of mountaineering in Yogistan.

This was a serious matter. There can be no doubt that the Yogistani is a natural mountaineer. When he becomes sufficiently civilized and educated to climb mountains voluntarily he may well be unapproachable. But so long as the initiative and the organizational responsibility rest with his Sahibs his undoubted powers must be kept under control. To reach the summit of Rum Doodle a partnership of brain and brawn was necessary; the brawn was indispensable, but it must be subordinated to the direction of the brain. We agreed that in future the porters should be restrained from endangering the health and safety of the party.

★

Before turning in that night I walked out to a small prominence above the camp to survey the view. The view was breathtaking. To the left North Doodle towered above the little camp, inhospitable and awe-inspiring. To the right the great shoulder of Rum Doodle itself soared above me, bleak and dreadful in the evening light. Below, on the glacier, Base Camp was a group of dots. The glacier wound away into the distance, losing itself among a

chaos of snow-capped peaks and pinnacles. To the
east a wilderness of desolation extended, peak after
mighty peak, as far as the eye could see. It was
breathtaking. Spires and pinnacles soared skyward
in profusion, taking one's breath away.

Breathless, I returned to my tent, to find Burley
already in his sleeping-bag and occupying three-
quarters of the floor space. I wriggled into the
remaining quarter as best I could, grateful for being
no bigger than I am. Burley and I were together at
last; I hoped that we would continue the confi-
dences of the afternoon.

We lay in silence for a while, then I suggested
that Burley might like to tell me about his fiancée.
He said why? and I thought I detected a reticence.
I said that talking about family and friends drew
men closer together. He said that since I put it like
that he didn't mind telling me; but it was not an
easy thing to talk about and I would understand
that he was not in the habit of chattering about it
to any busybody.

I said, of course, I quite understood, and would
value his confidence all the more on that account.
He told me that he had found his fiancée one
Saturday afternoon behind the sideboard in his
father's dining room. She was slight and small and
had a club-foot and a hare-lip and, consequently, a
limp and a lisp. She was near-sighted and carried an
ear-trumpet, being too nervous to use electrical
equipment to aid her deafness. She was either

colour-blind or had a bad memory for names. She was not very good-looking, but, as Burley said, one can't have everything. She had been studying the structure of the sideboard on behalf of the local antiquarian society, but had unfortunately got stuck and had been there a fortnight when Burley found her, being either too timid to call for help or too weak to make herself heard. Burley had rescued her single-handed, and this had been the turning-point of his life. He had, he said, realized at last his boyhood dream of rescuing a maiden in distress, and felt bound to fall in love with her. This he had done. She had, he said, many admirable qualities, which were none the less admirable for being hidden from the casual view. He himself was not sure what they were, which, besides giving him a sense of mystery and adventure, was proof of their delicacy. The finer qualities, he said, are never the obvious ones.

I said that I heartily agreed with him. I said also that I was touched by his story, which revealed a refinement which the unthinking would not think to find in one of his physique. I was moved to confess my affection for him and to express the hope that he and his fiancée would visit me at home.

His answer was a loud snore. Poor fellow, he must have been worn out. I made myself as comfortable as I could in my restricted space and occupied a sleepless night meditating on many things and looking forward to tomorrow's escape from Pong. Notwithstanding my discomfort it was one of the happiest nights I have ever spent. The expedition was going well; we were a united and happy party; the porters were splendid; I was with my friends. What more could a man want?

8

Advanced Base to Camp 2

The following day we regrouped. Wish had found some interesting ice which he wanted to boil, and stayed behind at Advanced Base with Burley, who was quite exhausted after his effort on the previous day and in no condition to go on. Constant and I were to escort the redundant porters back to Base Camp, returning next day. Jungle was to attempt to establish Camp 1 at 27,000 feet. Shute would follow Jungle after taking films of our various departures.

Shute had been up since dawn working on his apparatus, but it was still not operational when Jungle set off, nor an hour later when Jungle set off again, having gone round in a circle the first time. I noticed that neither of them passed any comment on the other's progress, and hoped that this was not a sign of altitude lassitude. But Jungle, when passing Shute the second time, made some remark about 'just swinging the compass', while Shute turned his handle as though taking shots. I hoped this did not indicate that they were trying to deceive each other; but I was too busy with my own affairs at the time to pay much attention. After getting ready Constant and I delayed our departure as long as we could, wishing to provide Shute with suitable material, but we were forced at last to set off unfilmed.

We reached Base Camp without incident and found Prone anaemic but cheerful. I spent the evening writing up my log and darning socks, while Constant confirmed with the porters the arrangements for moving the camp and assured me that these were thoroughly understood. It was with light hearts that we turned in for the night. Prone, with his usual unselfishness, refused to let me share his tent; he said that Constant and I, who would climb together, ought not to be parted. Constant was quite willing to let me go for one night, but I knew that Prone was right; Constant and I must lose no opportunity to learn more about each other. As it turned out, the only thing I was able to learn about Constant was that he was a good sleeper, for he dropped off as soon as I had settled down in my sleeping-bag.

We rose early, and I sent off the following despatch: 'North Wall conquered and reconnaissance of Rum Doodle begun. All well and happy and eager to come to grips with the mighty mountain which towers above us, daring us to set foot on her treacherous slopes. The team spirit remains first-rate and the porters are splendid.'

We said a final farewell to Prone. It was a deep disappointment to him – as indeed to all of us –

that he was unable to accompany us; and I wondered how his father would take the news of his incapacity. To his wife, no doubt, it would provide yet another means of tormenting the poor fellow. I did my best to cheer him up. I told him that the noble way in which he had borne his sufferings was a constant example and inspiration to us all, and especially to me, who knew his sad story. He patted me on the shoulder and said: 'Yes, little man.' He seemed quite pleased.

We reached Advanced Base without incident. Constant fell into several crevasses, and myself into one or two, but we were hauled out by the porters, who were learning quickly how to use the rope. Their names were So Lo and Lo Too. They were short and sturdy. When not smoking *stunk* – which was seldom – they quarrelled, or so it appeared to me, and they took absolutely no notice of Constant and myself except when we gave them orders, which they carried out meticulously but without the least sign of interest. Constant said that since we were now above the 20,000-feet line their dispositions would improve rapidly. I watched carefully for any sign of this happening, for, to tell the truth, I was somewhat overawed by their independence and impenetrability. I knew that the East is inscrutable, but I had hardly expected it to be inscrutable to my face.

We had reached a point some little distance up the first wall of ice, climbing by the steps we had used before, when Constant drew my attention to a small figure which was approaching us from the direction of Base Camp.

There are occasions when life hits a man so hard that he feels incapable of controlling his own destiny; he is like an insect crushed beneath the foot of a giant.

This was such an occasion for me, and I could see from Constant's face that he was equally stricken.

I dropped my eyes, hoping to forget what I had seen in his.

'Can nothing be done?' I whispered.

He shook his head. 'I'll try; but it's practically hopeless.'

The small figure was climbing the steps. It was bowed almost double beneath an immense pile of kitchen utensils which clanked and rattled at every step. It ascended towards us like a figure from the nether regions, stopping finally a few yards below and turning towards us a flat nightmare of a face.

Constant engaged it in a long and violent conversation, during which So Lo and Lo Too puffed away contentedly at their pipes, while I tried to regain control of my destiny by meditating on Totter's *Thoughts at High Altitudes*.

The wrangle came to an end at last, and Constant told me that he had been quite unable to persuade Pong to return; bribery, threats and deceit had all proved useless. Pong, he said, was evidently a man with a Purpose; short of throwing rocks at him, Constant could think of no possible way of turning him back. He had, however, told him that he should go no further than Advanced Base, where he would be needed to minister to anybody who might return from the mountain weak and helpless.

I said that this was rather hard on the weak and helpless. Constant agreed, but said he saw no alternative.

I thought for a while. The presence of Pong might endanger the whole expedition. Stomachs are delicate above 20,000 feet; specially attractive food had been incorporated in the high-altitude rations to tempt them. If Pong were to be let loose on the mountain health and hope might vanish. Was it not, perhaps, for Constant and myself to make the supreme sacrifice: to return to Base with Pong and suffer his ministrations in order to spare the rest of the team?

It was a great deal to ask of oneself. In the end I decided against it. We were needed on the mountain; we could not leave the others unsupported.

I slipped a dyspepsia tablet into my mouth and gave the word to advance.

We reached Advanced Base safely. It was deserted. I buzzed the walkie-talkie and made contact with Wish. Everybody was at Camp 1.

They would spend a day or two there to acclimatize before pushing on to Camp 2.

This was satisfactory news. I told him to expect Constant and myself tomorrow and got him to describe the route. While he was speaking I distinctly heard the strains of 'Oh, My Darling Clementine' being sung in the background, and I wished myself with the happy party.

I noticed afterwards that the medical supplies were missing and surmised that they had been taken to Camp 1. This puzzled me at the time. I gathered later that it had happened by mistake.

Our meal that evening was hardly as unsavoury as I had feared it would be, being merely indigestible. But Constant said that this was probably because Pong was not yet used to high-altitude rations; in his opinion the worst was yet to come. As it was, we were both unable to sleep, and I took the opportunity to make a few kindly enquiries about Constant's private life. I told him that it was not quite clear to me which of our party had fiancées and which had not, and I asked him if he had one. He said no. I asked him if his parents were still living. He said yes. I asked him if he had any brothers and sisters. He said yes. I told him I had three sisters. He said Oh.

There was something wrong here; nobody with a sense of atmosphere could be unaware of it. I lay for a while wondering how I might make contact with him and thinking how lonely is the human spirit, especially in grief. I suspected that Constant's taciturnity hid an aching heart.

This is the sort of situation which a conscientious leader often meets and is possibly the one case when it is kinder to ignore the other's feelings. Although it is difficult to speak of one's troubles it is always a relief; it is generally a greater kindness to make a sufferer speak of his sufferings than to respect his superficial desire to suffer them in silence.

The best way to invite a confidence is to give one. Guessing that Constant's reluctance was associated with an unhappy love affair I related to him an experience of my own which, although it caused me pain at the time, was now over and done with. I hoped that this would encourage him with the hope that his pain, too, would pass.

He made no comment on my story, so I remarked that such things happened to most of us.

Again, there was no reply. But I became aware of a peculiar sound, and on looking at Constant I saw that he was curled up in his sleeping-bag, quivering.

The poor fellow was sobbing!

Deeply moved, I put my hand on his shoulder. The sobbing became more violent.

'Tell me about it, old chap,' I said.

I thought he was going to lose control of himself altogether. But gradually the paroxysm passed. He turned over, and I saw that his cheeks were wet with tears.

'Tell me,' I said again.

He hastily covered his face as a few last sobs were wrenched from him. Then he lay quite still.

I could not help being aware that the atmosphere had changed, and I waited now in anticipation. I was not disappointed. He began to speak, slowly at first, hesitatingly; then with increasing fluency.

As a boy Constant had been a circus addict, and his passion, though discouraged by his parents, had continued throughout his life, changing only to mature with increasing age. His happiest memories were all connected with the circus; its peculiar blending of personality, grandiloquence and fantasy appealed to some deeply rooted romantic hunger. It was, he said, the same urge which dictated his choice of career. The people of the circus were to him more than ordinary people; they were at once his knights in armour, his fairies, his gnomes, his childhood princes and princesses. All his childish romances centred on the circus.

And his first and only love had been a circus artiste.

Her name was Stella. She performed with a troupe of seals. She was, said Constant, the loveliest creature in the world. Noblemen and princes worshipped her; but she was a simple girl at heart and would have none of them; she had vowed to marry a simple man and bear him simple children.

They loved at first sight and were happy as only first lovers can be. He saw her every performance; she kissed her hand to him twice nightly with matinées on Wednesdays and Saturdays.

There was but one flaw in the perfection of their private heaven. Travers, the chief male seal, took a dislike to Constant. Stella said it was jealousy. He barked whenever Constant approached her, and during performances he would come to the edge of the ring and pull faces at him, frightening the children. He began to refuse his food. The climax came when Stella walked on wearing Constant's engagement ring for the first time. When he saw it Travers uttered a cry which tore the hearts of all present. He flung himself on the ground and buried his face in his flippers.

Stella was heartbroken. She was greatly attached to her seals and felt their troubles as if they had been her children. She told Constant that she could not bear to hurt Travers any longer. She had, moreover, great faith in his judgment; his aversion to Constant might indicate some serious defect in character which was hidden to her. Unless he could make friends with the animal it must be all over between them.

Constant vowed he would do it. It was an adventure after his own romantic heart. He sent to all corners of the sea for fishy delicacies and spent all his leisure at Travers' tank, tempting him. But the poor animal remained unmoved. He would eat only from Stella's hand, and little enough at that. He became as thin as an eel.

Constant was frantic. He consulted authorities on seal psychology and visited ancient seamen in various hemispheres. He sat for hours in his bath trying to put himself in Travers' place. His toes became permanently wrinkled, but the secret of the seal's affection remained hidden from him.

One day, while strolling in the blackest despair through the West End of London, little caring what happened to him, he was seized by an uncontrollable impulse to justify his misery by performing some irretrievable act of degradation. Uttering a cry which changed the lives of three bystanders, he flung himself madly into a news cinema. A cartoon was just beginning. It opened with a rocky shore where a pretty mermaid was charming the creatures of the deep with a song. Amongst her audience was a large, healthy-looking seal which was listening with an expression of complete ecstasy. With a thrill, Constant saw that it was the image of Travers in his happier moments.

He dashed from the cinema and took a taxi straight to the circus, where he rushed to Travers' tank and laid bare his soul in a passionate rendering of 'Caller Herrin''.

The effect was startling. Lions roared, dogs howled, elephants trumpeted and stamped. An acrobat fell on his friend and three clowns gave their notice on the spot.

But Constant was oblivious to these trivia. For Travers was sitting up in the water with a smile of ultimate bliss, accompanying Constant in a well-modulated bass voice.

The circus manager rushed in and offered Constant a contract at a fabulous salary. Constant brushed him aside and hurried to Stella's dressing-room. Back they came together, and Constant and Travers continued their duet.

Stella gave a cry of love and flung herself at the ecstatic Constant. As she did so Travers gave a thunderous bellow. Astonished, she turned to the beast and tried to stroke its head. To her horror it bit her hand.

That was the end. The animal had transferred its affections to Constant and was insanely jealous of Stella. Heartbroken and furious, she told him to take the beast he had stolen and go. He clasped Travers in his arms and ran sobbing into the street, where he took a taxi to the zoo. All the time, Travers had continued to render his part of 'Caller Herrin".

Constant was sobbing again, his face hidden in his sleeping-bag. I waited until the fit had passed, then assured him of my deepest sympathy and said that I knew what a relief it must have been to tell me about it. He nodded. He was, he said, feeling better already. He had even begun to hope that he had at last conquered his grief.

I turned from him to wipe away a tear. The rewards of leadership are not always so immediate or so intense. When I had composed myself I asked him what had happened to Travers. The animal, he told me, had started a male voice choir among the zoo seals. Constant sang with them on Saturday afternoons.

★

That night both Constant and I slept badly. I had a recurring nightmare in which I saw Constant's face at the moment when he recognized Pong as the figure following us. But when it came closer it turned out to be a flat-faced seal which sobbed heartbrokenly and tried to hide itself in a sleeping-bag which was much too small for it. I awoke unrested. Constant was also tired out, having been seized with repeated bouts of sobbing which made the tent shake. He said they were due to habit and did not indicate grief any more, which was a comfort to me.

We were really in no condition to go on, but the mountain was less terrifying than the prospect of Pong's meals. We left him behind with great relief and assurances that we had never eaten so well in our lives. We told him that we would hurry back to partake as soon as possible of his culinary marvels. This, we assured him, would be the high spot of our adventure, the reward for difficulties surmounted, the silver lining to our cloud of toil. We begged him to stay where he was so as not to disappoint us.

We left him washing up and glowering.

We set off for Camp 1 by the route which Wish had described to us. Just above the Advanced Base a steep ridge rose for some 5,000 feet before merging into the face of the mountain. Our path lay up the left face of this ridge.

Constant and I were using oxygen. We found the apparatus so uncomfortable that we allowed So Lo to lead. The porters refused the aid of oxygen; I think they thought it was witchcraft.

After a short distance the ground steepened, and soon we – or rather the porters – were cutting steps in hard ice. We were now high. Every step climbed demanded an effort equivalent to running up 153 steps at sea level – the figure is Wish's. The great ordeal had begun at last. We could now number ourselves amongst those who had trod the ultimate heights and invaded nature's last stronghold against the advancing spirit of man.

I tried to remember all I had read about climbing at such heights. I took one step, then waited for ten minutes. This, I understood, was essential; our predecessors were unanimous about it: one step, then ten minutes' rest, or seven in an emergency. I found it more difficult than I had anticipated. To remain in one position for ten minutes was not at all easy. First, I tended to fall over sideways; then I got cramp in the calf; then my nose started to itch; then my foot started to vibrate and had to be held down by both hands. This was very tiring, and when I crouched to hold my foot I was lower than I had been before making the step, which caused me to wonder whether I was gaining height or losing it; and the mental strain was so great that I lost control of myself and fell off my step.

I was pulled up by So Lo, and tried again. I was beginning to appreciate all I had read concerning the rigours of high-altitude climbing. But I noticed that the others seemed to be ignoring the procedure. While I was struggling to maintain my posture they would shuffle about freely on their steps and even show signs of impatience. This I could understand in the case of the porters; but Constant, I thought, should know better. I was about to expostulate when he said: 'What on earth do you think you're doing, Binder?' I explained, and to my surprise he went off into fits of laughter. He said that the early climbers had been forced to rest after every few steps because they were out of breath. This was because they were not using oxygen. Nobody, he said, need rest any longer than he wanted to; at my rate of progress we should never get up the mountain.

This was a surprise to me, but after thinking it over it seemed quite reasonable, and I decided to give it a fair trial. I found to my delight that the going was not appreciably heavier than it had been the previous day. I mention this incident, in which I appear in no very admirable light, because it is a striking illustration of how one may be misled by book knowledge. It was a lesson to me, as a reader, to take nothing on trust, and as a writer to take the greatest care not to mislead my readers.

I hate to think what my progress might have been, had Constant not been there to put me right.

I soon found the going quite difficult enough, and I began to expect the onset of those strange phenomena which occur in rarefied atmospheres. I reminded Constant that I would like to hear of any unusual experiences he might have, and when we stopped for a rest I called the others on the radio and reminded them of the same thing. They were still at Camp 1, not yet acclimatized. Burley, to whom I spoke, told me that Wish was being particularly objectionable that morning; did I think this was one of the symptoms I was interested in? I assured him that it undoubtedly was, and thanked him. Wish apparently seized the apparatus at this point, for his voice now came through telling me that there was every reason for his attitude. Burley had snored heavily the whole night and Wish had been quite unable to get a wink. The snores, he said, were not, as he had expected, attenuated due to the rarefied atmosphere, but were much louder, more complicated and altogether more objection-able than they had ever been before. This, he said, was an example of how a man's true and bestial nature is revealed at high altitudes. Burley was clearly unfitted for social life above 20,000 feet – if, indeed, he could be considered fit for it at any altitude.

I commiserated with Wish, but asked him to be kind to his friend, who had much to bear. He promised to remember my words and asked me to keep a look-out for Wharton's warples.

Off we went again, climbing well, restraining the impetuous So Lo, who was inclined to rush the mountain – a fault to which all beginners are prone. A novice will tire himself out within an hour while the veteran keeps going all day at the same steady pace.

Higher and higher we climbed, and all the time our legs grew weaker and our breathing more laboured. It was now becoming necessary to stop quite often, but at first I found it almost a pleasure to stop because I had to and not because I *thought* I had to. The magnificent scenery around me had become much less interesting. I found myself concentrating on the seat of Constant's trousers – he being ahead of me. I thought I had never seen such a disgusting trousers' seat in all my life. I thought that Constant ought to be ashamed of himself for owning such a seat. I thought how different was the seat of Burley's trousers. I noted this down in my diary that evening as an interesting effect of high altitude.

We reached 27,000 feet in remarkably good

time, and looked around for Camp 1. To our dismay it was nowhere to be seen. I called up the others on the radio. Shute answered. I described to him as well as I could the route we had taken and the nature of our immediate surroundings. He said that as far as he could make out we were actually at Camp 1. He advised me to find some high spot from which we might get a good view. This was all very well, but the face of the ridge at this point was a maze of high spots; the tents might be hidden behind any one of a hundred crags or pinnacles. We reconnoitred and we shouted. We whistled and we yodelled. We exploded paper bags. All to no result.

We had just sat down to think it over when Constant gave a strangled cry and pointed downward.

Below, ascending by the steps we had cut, was a dark and grim figure.

Pong!

This was awful.

We held a hurried council of war. Pong was heavily laden. He seemed to have brought all the cooking equipment and most of the food we had left at Advanced Base. It was just possible that we could shake him off. We would abandon the search for Camp 1. We would climb as quickly and as high as we could and establish Camp 2 when we could go no further.

While we were talking Pong had drawn alarmingly close, and when we moved off I had to fight against unmanly panic. Constant said he had known nothing like it since being chased by a bull at Broadstairs on bank holiday.

We gave So Lo his head with the step-cutting and did our best to keep up with him. He set a tremendous pace. I doubt whether steps have ever been cut so quickly at any altitude. There was something unnatural about it. Mountaineering at 27,000 feet was supposed to be something almost superhuman; yet So Lo, without oxygen, was cutting steps as quickly as we, with oxygen, could climb them. It was all wrong; and it worried me. I was also worried about Constant's bull. It seemed to me very unlikely that there should be a loose bull at Broadstairs on bank holiday. Was Constant deceiving me? I also felt ashamed of myself for doubting him, which added to my worries.

In spite of our spanking pace Pong continued to gain on us. Faster and faster we went. Constant and I became dizzy and fell frequently. I became a mass of bruises, and Constant was in even worse condition; being taller than I he had further to fall. The climax came when, after a particularly bad fall, he found himself being picked up by Pong, who had caught us up. Constant uttered a horrid cry and collapsed, senseless. I revived him by hitting his head, and asked him what we should do. He said that since I was obviously in no condition to go on we had better camp where we were. This we did. I found that the height was 29,000 feet. We had established Camp 2 as originally planned. But this was small satisfaction to us at the time; we could think of nothing but the digestive horrors to come.

9

The Missing Camp

Sometimes, even now, I awake in the night screaming as I relive in dreams the misery of that wretched night. As soon as the tents were up Constant and I crept into our sleeping-bags and awaited supper. I prepared myself for the ordeal by thinking about Christian martyrs and reminding myself that Rum Doodle would hardly be worth climbing if it were no more than a pleasure trip. But my meditations were interrupted by a prolonged clattering which came from the direction of Pong's tent. Constant, whose nerve was beginning to go, went out to investigate. He came back trembling, with an ominous tale. Pong was crouched over a large stewpan, from which emerged indescribable odours. The ground in front of the tent was littered with empty food tins, and Constant had ascertained that their contents had been those special delicacies which we had chosen to attract the high-altitude palate. And when it appeared, the loathsome mess confirmed his forebodings. All our choicest titbits had gone into Pong's awful pot: our luscious breast of chicken, the tinned apricots and cream which we had so often tasted in anticipation, the sardines, the caviar, the lobster, the lovely gruyère cheese, the pickled walnuts, the curry, the salmon, even the coffee and the chocolate biscuits: all these were reduced to a nauseating brew which might have sent Macbeth's witches shrieking from the place.

The horrors of that meal were but the prelude to a night such as few human beings can have endured. It was, I think, about midnight when I awoke from a nightmare in which I was buried under Rum Doodle, to find Constant lying across my chest snoring heavily and muttering. When I pushed him off he awoke with a cry of terror and hit me on the nose, making my eyes water. I apologized for waking him, and we settled down again. I must have dozed off, for I awoke suddenly under the impression that a prehistoric monster had crept into the tent and was about to do me an injury. I seized the nearest solid object – which happened to be a climbing boot – and hit the monster as hard as I could. It was Constant, of course. I asked had I woken him; and if he said what I thought he said he is not the man I think he is. I decided after careful thought that I must have imagined it, and was just dropping off again when Constant uttered a wild cry and bit me in the ear. I woke him up and suggested that it might be safer to sleep head to foot. After some strange remarks he agreed, and I started to shuffle around in my sleeping-bag. It was breathless work at that altitude.

I had to stop three times to rest, and when I finally completed the turn I found that I had lost my pillow on the way. I could not face the thought of searching for it, so I made a boot do instead.

I was almost asleep again when a horrid noise sounded a few inches from my face. Terrified, I struck out instinctively, and found myself grasping, of all things, a mouth. This was quite horrible; I don't think I shall ever forget the alarm and disgust which it caused me. We found out later that we had both turned round together and were still sleeping head to head. Waking suddenly out of the nightmare caused by the clutch on his mouth, Constant flung himself upon me. Still dazed by sleep and terror I fought back madly, and we were wrestling all over the tent. I was soon exhausted, and had almost given up hope of surviving when Constant stopped suddenly and lay where he was, panting. When we had recovered our breath and wits I apologized again, and we tried to disentangle ourselves. But this was not as easy as one might expect. We were locked in a complicated embrace, half in and half out of our sleeping-bags, with ropes and clothing wrapped around us. It was pitch dark. In the middle of the operation I dropped off to sleep in a sitting position, to wake screaming under the impression that the rope was a snake which was trying to strangle me. I struggled desperately with the rope before I came to my senses, making the tangle ten times worse.

We went to it again, but somehow we could never make each other understand what we were trying to do. Sometimes we would be pulling in opposite directions on the same section of rope; sometimes we would roll over and get our legs entangled; sometimes we would strike out in a bold bid to free an arm, and catch each other in the eye. We were continually out of breath. Every other minute one of us would be seized with cramp or stomach-ache and writhe about, making it all worse than ever. We kept falling asleep and waking terrified after the most hideous nightmares.

Finally, the tent came down on us.

After that we gave it up. We just stayed where we were and waited for daylight.

When it was light enough to see we got our heads out somehow and looked at each other.

'This can't go on,' said Constant.

This, I thought, was very well put. At all costs we must get down to Camp 1.

But first we had to get out of the tent, which was no light matter at 29,000 feet. After a few moments of struggle we were forced to stop to regain our breath. Our hands were freezing; we had to put on gloves, which made the job of disentangling almost impossible. At one point I almost gave up in despair. I lay gasping, with Constant sitting on my head, my arms bound behind me with rope, my legs wrapped in tent and sleeping-bag. For the third time I faced the possibility of defeat. Was the mountain too strong for us, after all?

To make matters worse, Pong came with breakfast.

After a sharp and manly struggle with nausea, Constant sent Pong for So Lo and Lo Too. Soon they were working on us, and at last, after what seemed an eternity, we were free men.

Telling the porters to re-erect the tent we retired to theirs, where we spent some time boiling our boots in order to de-ice them. Pong followed us with breakfast, which was a rehash of yesterday's left-overs made still more deplorable by burning. We forced ourselves to swallow a few mouthfuls, holding our noses and closing our eyes and telling ourselves that it was for the sake of the expedition. Then we took some stomach tablets and made our plans. They were simple. We must make Camp 1 as quickly as possible and spread the burden of Pong as widely as we could.

We radioed the others and told them to expect us; but we said nothing about Pong, not daring to risk a panic on the mountain. Jungle told me that they would wait for us. Burley, he said, had just become acclimatized but thought that a further day at Camp 1 would consolidate his fitness. The others, too, thought they would benefit from an extra day of rest.

We moved off early. Our wet boots froze immediately; short of a rise in temperature, nothing but an amputation could have separated us from them. We fell all over the place and sometimes went to sleep where we lay. So Lo and Lo Too kept saving our lives; but at last they seemed to get tired of it, for they threw us on top of their loads and carried us for the rest of the day.

At 27,000 feet we cast about once more for Camp 1, and again, in spite of radioed instructions, we failed to find it. In desperation we decided to make for Advanced Base. We reached it in the late afternoon as exhausted as two men could possibly be.

Our first job was to thaw off our boots. This we did by putting our feet in a bucket of melted snow which we then boiled over a pressure stove. Luckily, spare boots were available. We then put a short call through to Camp 1 and went straight to bed, refusing food and drink.

★

Next day we were somewhat recovered. Under normal circumstances we should have taken a long rest, but since this would mean remaining at Pong's mercy it was not to be thought of. During the night we had crept into the mess tent and snatched a little food. Fortified by this we were able to deny ourselves breakfast, and we set off for Camp 1 shortly after sunrise. We made no attempt this time to leave Pong behind. He had by now demoralized us completely; even to refuse a meal was an act requiring the combined moral courage of both of us.

We had been somewhat cheered to learn that Shute, Jungle and Wish had already started for Camp 2. Burley, now alone at Camp 1, had unfortunately passed the peak of his acclimatization and had deteriorated during the previous day. He thought it advisable to stay behind and recuperate.

The day's climb was strenuous but uneventful. Neither Constant nor myself was fit for anything but a dogged trudge behind the porters. Ever since we had been above 20,000 feet I had been expecting the improvement in their disposition which Constant had promised. It never came. To the end they remained obedient and hard-working but completely independent and unapproachable. Constant said he could not understand this, but thought that perhaps they were not Yogistanis at all, but Rudistanis, who were a different kind of people altogether. He said he would look it up in his correspondence-course notes when he got back home.

At 27,000 feet we made our usual search, with the usual result. To this day I am utterly unable to account for our repeated failure to locate Camp 1.

Tired though we were, we had no alternative but to make for Camp 2. It was a pity to leave Burley alone at Camp 1, but I consoled myself with the thought that there would now be five of us to share the burden of Pong. Our combined wits might devise some method of circumventing him.

So it was onwards and upwards again. Using the steps we had cut two days before we mounted quickly, and Camp 2 was reached without further incident.

★

Constant and I had been miserable for so long that it was almost with surprise that we found happy people at Camp 2. As we drew near, the strains of 'Roll Out The Barrel' charmed us like the Hosannas of the Blessed.

We were welcomed with open arms and hearty back-slappings. We were punched and thumped. Our hair was ruffled. We were tripped and sat upon. Snow was put down our necks. Our bootlaces were tied together so that we fell flat on our faces.

I had not seen my comrades so boisterous since the crevasse incident. I wondered what the cause might be.

And then they saw Pong.

I have never seen a mood change so suddenly. The heaviest depression descended upon us like a plague of Egypt. The three who, one short moment before, had been as gay as sandboys, shrank into melancholy like old men. They glowered at each other and snarled maledictions. They wrung their hands and shook their heads continually. They muttered. They slunk into their tents and cowered in the corners, biting their nails and drooling. They cried quietly when no one was looking.

Coming on top of my long ordeal it was too much for me. I crept supperless into my sleeping-bag and sobbed myself to sleep.

★

I awoke next morning to find Constant sitting up in his sleeping-bag. His face was drawn.

'They've gone!' he said.

'You mean?' I gasped.

He nodded.

'Tell me,' I pleaded.

His whole frame quivered with a deep, searing sigh. His mouth opened and a long moan was forced through a tortured throat as he strained to tell the horror of it.

'Betrayed!' he groaned.

'You mean?' I said.

He nodded.

It was awful.

Gradually, I soothed him; and as the friendly sun mounted in the heavens, warming our little tent, he gathered courage. Once, when the shadow of the prowling Pong fell across the tent roof, he screamed; but soon manhood reasserted itself and he was telling me his story in a voice whose gentleness was infinitely poignant.

Jungle and Wish had crept away before dawn

and fled up the mountain. Shute had left soon afterwards on his way back to Camp 1.

★

For the whole of that day we lay in our sleeping-bags, each facing the crisis in his own way. Towards evening, Constant spoke. 'Tomorrow,' he said, 'I go down to Camp 1.'

I nodded. It was inevitable. I turned over and slept.

Next morning I awoke to find him gone. I was not surprised. I was not disappointed. I was hardly even interested. This was the end: the end of high endeavour, the end of comradeship, the end of dreams, the end of life itself. I stood on the brink of an infinite nothingness. Without a sigh, without a backward glance, resignedly, even thankfully, I stepped over the threshold.

★

Somebody was slapping my face in a most unpleasant manner. An impatient voice was saying: 'Wake up, Binder, you silly fool!'

I woke, opened my eyes, and looked around me.

I was lying on my back on the snow, in full and blinding daylight. Shute was bending over me.

'Where am I?' I said.

'Where do you think you are?' he asked.

I considered this for a while.

'I thought I might be in heaven,' I said.

He roared with laughter. 'I say, chaps: Binder thinks he's in heaven!'

More laughter. I looked around. Wish was there, and Jungle; and, seated on a box beside me, looking very weary, Constant.

And behind them, peering down at me, were several porters, including So Lo, Lo Too and Pong.

Then I saw the tents and began to get my bearings. It was Camp 2. Constant and I had just arrived from Advanced Base for the second time, finding the others in possession. I must have fallen asleep. The rest had been a dream.

Higher than Everest

After a meal which is better left undescribed we crowded into one small tent to discuss future plans. The question was: what were we to do about Pong? Several suggestions were made, but none was both practical and humane. Wish summed up in his precise way, saying that we must accept Pong as one of the hazards of the mountain and make our plans accordingly.

Constant said that he and I had had Pong for four days and it was somebody else's turn. Wish said that, in principle, he was entirely in agreement with this, but we must see how it worked out in practice. We must, he said, assume that when we split up, Pong would attach himself to the larger party in order to do the maximum amount of damage. But he could be thwarted in this by a simple stratagem. We were now five. In the morning, two would move off together to establish Camp 3, leaving three at Camp 2. Pong would naturally stay with these three. But shortly afterwards one of the three would leave, either for Camp 3 or to return to Camp 1. Again, Pong would stay with the majority. Later on, the remaining two would split, so that Pong's sphere of influence would be reduced to one.

'Isn't that rather hard on the last man?' I asked.

'It's only for a short while,' Wish assured me. 'We can change round later to suit circumstances. Is it agreed, then?'

Constant and I glanced at each other doubtfully. But Shute and Jungle said that it was a perfect scheme, and congratulated Wish on his masterly command of strategy.

'Very well,' he said. 'Now, it's obvious that Binder and Applecart are in no condition to go up to Camp 3.'

'Agreed,' said Shute and Jungle.

'In fact,' Wish continued, 'it is essential that they take a day's rest.'

'Absolutely,' said Shute and Jungle.

'So they must stay here with Pong.'

'Nothing else will do,' said Shute and Jungle.

'And now for the others,' said Wish. 'I take it that you two don't want to go together?'

'Certainly not,' said Shute and Jungle. I wondered why.

'So I shall go to Camp 3 with one of you. Which is it to be?'

'Jungle,' said Shute.

'Shute,' said Jungle.

'You'd better toss for it,' Wish suggested.

'Heads,' said Shute.

'It's tails,' said Jungle.'

'Congratulations, old boy,' said Shute. 'You'll be the first to go higher than Everest.'

'But I won,' said Jungle.

'Well of course you did. The loser stays behind.'

'But I thought it was the other way round.'

'Why ever should it be?' said Shute.

'Well . . .' said Jungle.

'Of course,' Shute went on, 'if you think I'm trying to diddle you . . .'

Jungle said nothing.

'You don't trust me.'

Jungle hung his head.

'After all I've done for you.'

Jungle wriggled.

'Very well,' said Shute. 'We'll toss up again. Heads.'

'Heads it is,' said Jungle.

'My choice,' said Shute. 'I didn't like to mention it before, but I'm not feeling quite up to the mark. I daren't risk letting the side down. I will go back to Camp 1.'

Jungle looked a little bewildered. He withdrew from the conversation and sat for quite a long time with puckered brow, muttering to himself and counting off points on his fingers. From time to time he would open his mouth to speak, then think better of it. Finally, he gave a deep sigh and became quite still, staring at nothing like one who had given up all hope and was quietly waiting for death. I scented undercurrents, but I was too tired to investigate. Besides, I had other worries: how were Constant and I to endure another day at the mercy of Pong?

I put the problem to Wish, and that master-strategist produced a workable plan. Someone must decoy Pong out of the cooking tent so that someone else could steal some food, which would be concealed in the sleeping-bags of Constant and myself. Tomorrow we would live on this store, telling Pong we required no meals. We would thus have a whole day to recover our digestion. Wish suggested that those travelling with Pong should take only the plainest food, upon which his black art would have the least effect.

This was agreed upon. It was hard to forgo the dainties which we had looked forward to for so long, but it was better than having them reduced to the sickening messes which Constant and I had already endured.

The raid on the larder was organized. Jungle was sent outside to hide behind a cliff; then Constant called Pong into our tent and engaged him in conversation. They had exchanged only a few gurgles when Pong moved his head as though listening to a faint sound. The next moment he rushed from the tent and we heard him bellowing as he ran towards his kitchen.

We all hurried outside, to see Jungle flying down the mountain with Pong after him.

Wish, quick-witted as ever, dashed into the

kitchen and emerged with an armful of food of various kinds. He ran straight to our tent with it; and it was lucky he did so, for Pong abandoned the chase suddenly and hurried back to the kitchen, where he squatted in the doorway glowering at us.

Jungle was now out of sight, and the general opinion was that we should never see him again. There was nothing else for it: a search-party must be organized. The porters were sent after him, while the rest of us stood by ready to defend him, with our lives if need be, against another attack.

It was two hours before the search-party returned, Jungle being carried on the back of a small but sturdy porter. Pong made no move, and we went back to our tent in peace.

Tired though I was I considered it my duty to acquaint myself with everything that had transpired since our last meeting at Advanced Base five days before. In his two days at Camp 1, Wish had melted thirteen hundredweight of ice and recalibrated his thermometers. Shute had run off two thousand feet of film and, had the lid not been accidentally knocked off his dark box, exposing the contents to daylight, some very fine sequences would have resulted. Jungle had swung his compasses higher than compasses had ever been swung before; those which survived were to be considered accurate within certain limits which he was unable to determine.

We called Burley on the walkie-talkie and

learned that he was still recuperating and did not consider it advisable to move from Camp 1 just yet.

Finally, I asked if anybody had any unusual experiences to report. The response was most interesting. Both Wish and Shute had experienced high-altitude hallucinations. Wish had seen differential equations, test-tubes and Wimshurst machines, while Shute had been frightened by a vision of a camera obscura. Jungle had shown a tendency to wander when not roped to the others. He had also become convinced that he was being followed by a Prude. When asked what a Prude was he became confused. Wish said: 'Nice going, Wanderer,' as if Jungle were somehow responsible for the Prude, and they all burst out laughing. I must say the point, if any, of the joke escaped me; I daresay they were suffering from altitude hysteria.

We turned in a happy and united party, and in spite of Pong's supper I spent a reasonably comfortable night.

★

Next morning we were astir early. Jungle and Wish went off without breakfast, intending to stop for a meal as soon as they were out of sight of Pong. They took with them all the tasty food, leaving us only lentils and pemmican, which were considered to be the most Pong-proof of our supplies, being naturally unappetizing. Shute departed shortly afterwards with his one porter, leaving Constant and me with So Lo, Lo Too and Pong. We went back to our sleeping-bags, where we stayed all day, feeding ourselves on cold food and hiding the debris. In the early evening we had a call from Shute, who was safely back at Camp 1 with Burley. Burley, he said, had fully recuperated and considered himself reclimatized. He had, however, contracted sleeping-bag lassitude and did not feel justified in setting out just yet.

Wish called shortly afterwards. He and Jungle had had a hard day, but they had reached the point where the ridge on which we were climbing merged with the face of the mountain, and had established Camp 3 at 31,000 feet. Fixed ropes had been left in the difficult places. He had seen some more differential equations and two filter funnels and heard three retorts. Jungle had shown a tendency to walk backwards.

★

We rose betimes the following morning. Our private store of food had given out and we were forced to breakfast on lentils and pemmican prepared by Pong. Constant took one mouthful and turned pale. 'I'm sorry, old boy,' he said. 'I just can't face it. I must go down to Camp 1.'

This was sad news, but hardly surprising. We parted regretfully; we had been through much together. I told Constant that the manly way in which he had borne his sufferings had been a continual inspiration to me, and that I would treasure the memory of the six days we had spent together. Constant said that he, too, would not forget in a hurry.

Constant took Lo Too, leaving me So Lo and Pong. I let So Lo take the lead, wishing to conserve my mental energies. I was on the look-out for altitude hallucinations and warples. Several times I thought I saw a warple, but it turned out to be a hallucination. Several times I thought I saw a hallucination, but it turned out to be a spot on my goggles. Once I thought I saw a spot on my goggles, but it turned out to be a warple which turned out to be a hallucination. To keep my stomach-ache under control I had taken little breakfast, and was weak with hunger. I fed myself with dyspepsia tablets, which gave me a headache. I found by accident that licking the glacier-cream off my face gave my stomach some relief. Unfortunately, this resulted in both sunburn and a frozen tongue, and when I put my tongue back in my mouth to thaw it gave me toothache. I was also worried because most of my dream had come true. My four companions had dispersed exactly as they had done in the dream, which seemed sinister.

All this interfered with the rhythm which is so essential to climbing at high altitudes. I decided to forget everything else and concentrate on the rhythm. I devised a little rhyme to keep step with my feet:

> *Organ grinders, kings and queens*
> *Call for Binder's Butter Beans.*

Three times daily, knave and noodle
*Eat them gaily on Rum Doodle.**

This went round and round in my brain all day, and made such a nuisance of itself that it only added to my worries. I began to fear that I was about to lose control of my destiny.

Luckily, we reached Camp 3 before this happened. Still in control of my destiny, I greeted Wish and Jungle, who were having a rest day. In anticipation of meeting Pong again they had already dined, and they managed to keep their stores out of his reach. I dined alone on lentils and pemmican.

I was tired out, but happy in the thought that I should soon be relieved of Pong. But somehow it turned out quite differently. Using the anti-Pong strategy which, Wish said, had worked so well at Camp 2, Wish decided that one of us must go off alone in the morning, leaving Pong with the majority of two. Later, one of these would go, leaving Pong with the last man. Since I needed a rest, I must be that last man.

Wish was very nice about it. He said I had his deepest sympathy. He said that, if anything, he was more upset about it than I was. He said that only the strictest sense of duty restrained him from insisting on taking Pong himself, whatever I might say. He said that he had never felt so acutely the

---

* This was not true.

conflict between personal desire and the welfare of
the expedition. He said that I would understand.

I said I did indeed, and felt his distress as deeply
as he did himself. I begged him to put a brave face
on it and let duty be its own reward. He thanked
me and said that he would not forget my words. It
was with a sense of deep humility that I wished
him good-night and went to my lonely tent.

★

And so, next morning, Wish started first, taking
one porter, on an attempt to establish Camp 4.
Jungle said he had deteriorated badly and must at
all costs go down to Camp 1 to recuperate. While
he was waiting for the day to warm up I tried to
persuade him to talk about himself, and was at last
able to say tactfully that I understood he had no
fiancée. He said that this was the case, and I said
that no doubt one of his roving disposition was not
naturally disposed to bind himself with home ties.
He surprised me by saying that, on the contrary, he
felt deeply the need for a home and a loved one.
He reminded me that every bird has its nest and
every expedition its base. He was in the unhappy
position of being, as it were, an expedition without
a base, a bird without a nest. During his wanderings, he consoled his lonely heart with dreams of
finding its desire. He liked to think that some day,
over the brow of some distant hill, he would find
his spiritual home; in a small but well-built cottage,

with modern plumbing, he would find the soul-
mate who had waited faithfully for the lover she
had dreamed of for so many lonely years. His
wanderings, he said, were all *towards* somewhere;
but where he did not know; this was why he had
sometimes been known to lose his way.

I said that I was touched by his confidence. I said
I knew very well how he felt, having myself been a
wanderer in my younger days. I asked Jungle
whether he had never found a young lady to his
taste. He said yes, he had found quite a number; in
fact, he was always finding them. He said that,
unfortunately, he lost them as quickly as he found
them. He was in the habit of taking them on
excursions on Saturday afternoons, and almost
invariably mislaid them. He had lost three in
succession on the South Downs. On the first
occasion they had been overtaken by mist and
Jungle had instructed his lady to remain where she
was while he went for help. He took a northerly
course until he reached a farm, then returned due
south with a search party. The silly girl must have
moved, for they were unable to find her. I asked
him whether she had reached home safely. He said
that he had not enquired; a girl who moved about
in a mist against orders was hardly worth enquiring
about. The next lady disappeared while Jungle was
swinging his compass. The third became annoyed
when Jungle inadvertently led her in a circle, and

walked off. He had lost several in the Underground, two or three in Waterloo station, and any number in Hampton Court maze.

I made the friendly suggestion that next time, having found his lady, Jungle might keep hold of her and refrain from wandering. He said that he had often decided to do this, but it didn't seem to be in his nature. He was, he said, the victim of a Destiny. It was his Fate to go on finding his heart's desire and losing it, wandering about the face of the earth, forever homeless and lonely.

I said that this was the very stuff of Tragedy. It was so poetic that it must be true. I begged Jungle to think of himself as one chosen to fulfil a high and stern purpose; to put away weak desires and accept his Calling.

He thanked me and said that he would try to do as I suggested. He said that his earthly consolation should be that, himself a wanderer, he might sometimes be granted the privilege of guiding others.

At this point Pong brought his midday meal, and Jungle departed hurriedly for Camp 1 with his porter.

Left alone, I tried to meditate upon the responsibilities of leadership, but so weakened were my powers of concentration that I could think of nothing but apricot jam. Camp 1 was out of radio range, but in the evening I had a conversation with Wish, who had established Camp 4 at 33,000 feet.

This was indeed good news; it cheered me so much that I was able, with no effort at all, to think of plum jam and marmalade. I asked Wish whether he liked plum jam. I think he thought I was light-headed.

Higher Still

I was sufficiently rested next day to set out for Camp 4, which was visible just below the skyline, a single small black dot in a white wilderness. I was now on the face of the mountain itself and the ground was steeper than it had been on the ridge and swept by an icy wind.

I moved slowly. My knees trembled; my feet turned to ten past ten; I frequently fell on my face. This, added to the fact that I no longer felt a strong desire to look for warples, led me to suspect that I was weakening. I found that my thoughts would rise no higher than my stomach or the next step, whichever was the lower. I was losing control of my destiny and the expedition.

This would never do. When the leader gives up the team falls to pieces. Who knew what struggles were going on below me? Was I to be the one to fail the party?

No, I said; I would not fail. I said it was time I stopped feeling sorry for myself. I had been telling myself that I was miserable, and, being a naturally truthful person, I had believed myself. The remedy was plain: I must tell myself something cheerful.

I told myself that my knees were firm and my feet straight. I told myself that I was gaining strength with every step. I said that my stomach-ache was hardly worth thinking about. I said I was all eagerness to find warples.

I talked to myself all day. I think I was on the point of convincing myself when, sometime in the late afternoon, I fancied my eyes were getting weak and began to fear snow-blindness. I told myself that it was all imagination. I tried hard to convince myself of this, and it did at last seem that my eyes were improving. But when we reached Camp 4 I found that my goggles had frosted over.

I found Wish in residence. He gave me a long and interesting list of the scientific apparatus he had seen during the previous day's climb. He kept me quite busy writing it all down. I would reproduce the list here; but it is not likely to be of general interest, being very like a manufacturer's catalogue.

I told Wish that I intended to spend one day at Camp 4 to acclimatize, then push on as quickly as possible in order to make maximum height before my strength gave out. I said I hoped he would accompany me.

Wish said that that was exactly what he himself would have liked to do. Unfortunately, he had deteriorated during his stay at Camp 4 and must go down to recuperate. He added that this would probably enable him, from Camp 3, to relay messages between myself at Camp 4 and those lower down. It was, he said, essential to make contact with the others, and this was the only practicable way of doing it.

I hope that I am not being self-indulgent when I ascribe to the effects of altitude my temporary irritation with Wish's logical conclusions. I recognized the truth of what he said, but it seemed to me at the time that Truth and Wish had ganged up against me. This was ungracious of me, particularly in view of Wish's sympathy in a similar situation at Camp 3.

After a frugal supper of lentils and pemmican I found myself sufficiently restored to make inner amends to Wish. This put me in the mood for a good talk, and, Wish being a scientist and used to dealing directly with truth, I saw no harm in confessing outright my interest in the matrimonial state of the party and asking him if he himself had a fiancée. He replied that it was an interesting point. I said yes, it was, and then we fell silent. After a while I reminded him that he had not answered my question and said I hoped he had not taken offence at anything I might have said. He said no, on the contrary; he was touched by my interest. The fact was, it was not quite clear to him either. I said I would be very happy if he would confide in me. He then told me his story, but slowly and with difficulty. Poor fellow, his emotion was so strong that the words did not come easily.

He had, he said, always wanted a fiancée. Even

as a child it had been his heart's desire. He always asked Father Christmas to send him one, and repeated disappointments had caused him to develop at an early age a sense of disillusion which many a mature man might have envied. When he discovered that Father Christmas did not in fact exist he decided in his small mind that he could no longer place any trust in his parents. From this it was but a short step to doubting everything that was told him. By his sixth birthday he was a complete sceptic.

He asked me if I could understand his feelings. I said yes; a sensitive and intelligent child might easily react in this way. I myself had long had doubts about the advisability of Father Christmas, and Wish's experience was of great interest to me. I begged him to continue.

At the age of seven he asked his father to tell him the facts of life, with particular reference to fiancées. But he found it quite impossible to believe what was told him; it seemed to him, he said, much more unlikely than Father Christmas. In great bewilderment he consulted some of his small friends who, equally puzzled, approached their own parents on the subject. The explanations they brought to him were so varied and contradictory that the poor child was confirmed in his opinion that the whole thing was just another fairy-tale. He became convinced that fiancées were no more real than Father Christmas.

The parents of his small friends had become alarmed by the sudden outbreak of interest in this delicate subject. Having discovered the author, they held a meeting and, after much careful thought, they clubbed together and bought the boy a catapult, hoping that it would take his mind away from other things.

Except for the additional expense of broken windows they were quite satisfied with the result. The boy's natural delight at owning a weapon of destruction drew his attention away from the subject of fiancées, thus relieving an inner tension which might well have resulted in a political career.

Some years later, during his student days, his interest in the subject was reawakened by a chance remark made by a servant girl. By consulting works of reference and talking to many authorities he acquired an exhaustive knowledge of current beliefs. But his scepticism was still more robust than his credulity. In spite of a strong and self-confessed desire to believe he found it impossible to do so. It seemed, he said, that he alone of the human race was able to see the uncomfortable truth, to stand outside the cosy glow of illusion. He began to believe that his mission in life was to disclose to mankind the light which had revealed itself to him alone. He spoke eloquently and often in discussion and debate and founded a group known as 'Whence?' whose motto was 'Whither?' He even wrote a monograph entitled *Fiancées: The Pathetic Myth* which was published by the Sensible Press at 3½d. and remaindered in ten editions.

He was send down from university for steadfastly refusing to believe anything which was taught him. The Whencians gave him a public send-off and proclaimed him the first martyr of the new lack of faith. But having come down he found, as many a young man had found before him, that the world of men and affairs was a vastly different place from the world of his imaginings. His first rude awakening occurred one Saturday afternoon in the saloon bar of *The Psychic Psquirrel*. Wish had been holding forth in his usual way and had, he thought, expounded his Theory of Scepticism with particular clarity and brilliance. When he had finished, an elderly, rather disreputable-looking gentleman of the eccentric type spoke a few quiet sentences which quite removed Wish's self-satisfaction. He said he would not deny that Wish showed certain faint glimmerings of promise as a sceptic. But he had far to go. He must learn the elementary truth that the real sceptic is sceptical by character rather than conviction; the intellectual drapery in which he clothes his scepticism has as little importance as the demonstrations of the believer – it is, indeed, more likely to veil than to reveal the naked Truth. Moreover, knowing that his mind will enable him to doubt everything, the sceptic scorns the crudity of *stating* his disbelief; he merely *lives* it. But even this, the gentleman said, was going too far. The true sceptic would refuse even to believe in himself and his own scepticism. He would maintain an openness of mind indistinguishable from complete mindlessness and an openness of character indistinguishable from utter lack of character. His scepticism would find its ultimate expression in the acceptance of random prejudice as being as sound a basis for living as the most carefully reasoned philosophy. This, he said, was the ultimate faith, for it scorned intellectual pretext. He said that the true sceptic was far stronger in faith than any believer.

Wish left *The Psychic Psquirrel* a very confused man. He spent a wretched night and awoke with a violent headache and a strong prejudice against alcoholic refreshment in any form and casual conversation with eccentric strangers.

This prejudice was the turning-point in his life. There was, he said, no arguing about it; sense or nonsense, it was completely convincing to him. This was a revelation. He reasoned that since he must live by prejudice he might as well choose the most comfortable ones he could find. He started to look around, scrutinizing carefully every prejudice he came across, no matter how worn or dilapidated it might appear. He examined thousands: some soft and comfortable, some sharp and excruciating; prejudices large, prejudices small; prejudices personal, national, harmless, deadly, ancient, modern,

scientific, superstitious, plebeian, aristocratic, practical, useless, orthodox, heretical: prejudices galore
and free for the taking. He felt, he said, like an
explorer who comes upon a treasure-chest
crammed with the richest and most beautiful gems.

He picked here and there, deliberately, taking
his time. He chose a complete set of prejudices
which would last him a lifetime and fit him to deal
with any situation. He chose his career. He joined
a political party.

The pride of his collection was his old heart's
desire: the craving for a fiancée. Prejudice had
restored what reason had banished. Happily, rever-
ently, with a feeling of miracles performed, he put
it back in its old place.

It didn't fit.

He turned it this way and that. He examined it
for wear. He reasoned with himself and read long
passages from text books. He lied to himself. He
took advice from anybody who would tell him
what he wanted to hear.

All in vain!

Wish said he wondered if I could appreciate his
feelings. He had, he said, convinced himself
beyond all reasonable doubt that the popular view
was the correct one. He could prove it to himself
by every known intellectual test. Moreover, he
wanted to believe it. In a sense, he *did* believe it; but
not completely. There was always a reserve at the
back of his mind, and as time went on this emerged

as a conviction that the whole thing was a plot to deceive him: a vast plot which included the writers of books and Wish's own friends.

He asked me if I thought him over-fanciful. I said that, on the contrary, I found it extremely interesting, having myself had an experience very similar to his, though perhaps less intense. It happened while I was on my way to Scotland to join some friends for a climbing holiday. Half-way up the Great North Road – I was travelling by bicycle – I began to suspect that Scotland did not exist: that it had been invented just to make a fool of me. All the books I had read, all the stories about thrifty Scotsmen, Shakespeare's Macbeth, Rabbie Burns, songs about Loch Lomond and Bonnie Charlie: all these were part of the conspiracy. The northerners who pretended to come from Scotland were all in the plot; their accent had been invented for the purpose. I was almost convinced that at Berwick-on-Tweed I should be laughed at by thousands of practical jokers whose entire lives had been devoted to bringing about this one ridiculous event. I became so apprehensive that I was unable to continue my journey by cycle. I thought that if I went by train I should avoid exposure; for if Scotland really did not exist the Railway Company would certainly know about it and would not issue a ticket. But when I got to the booking office I realized that if this was the case I should look just as foolish trying to buy a ticket as if I tried to cycle to

Scotland – with no possible chance of pretending that I had really no intention of going further than the border. I realized too that if there actually was a conspiracy the Railway Company would be in it and would have false tickets ready at every booking office in case I came along. But it was too late to turn back. I bought a ticket to Berwick, and was almost sure that the clerk looked disappointed. Once on the train I made discreet enquiries of officials and my fellow travellers, besides examining labels on the luggage van, and decided that if it was all part of the conspiracy it was a remarkably thorough business. I decided that Scotland was a calculated risk worth taking. At Berwick I left the train and cycled over the border.

Wish said that this was exactly the sort of thing he had experienced in regard to fiancées. Unfortunately, he had been able to find no easy solution such as mine. Shortly after the encounter at *The Psychic Psquirrel* he met a young person who, he said, was exactly the kind of person he would have wished to have as a fiancée if he could have persuaded himself to believe in them. So strong were his feelings that he decided to risk exposure by asking her to be his. To his great delight she promised to do so.

This occurred just before we left England. For a few days Wish was the happiest mountaineer alive. His dearest childhood dream was realized. He was almost ready to believe in Father Christmas.

Then came Doubt. *Was* it true? *Could* it be true? Was his fiancée, perhaps, in the conspiracy? Would he, on our return home, be exposed to a nation's ridicule?

Since then he had been torn between Love and Fear, and had not known a moment's peace. Nobody, he said, could possibly imagine the torments he had borne.

He groaned in a most distressing way. Poor fellow! I tried to reassure him that his fears were all fancies; but what could I do against the scepticism of a lifetime? I told him I would not be happy until I had put his mind at ease. I begged him to let me share his thoughts and help him in his struggle. He was pathetically grateful, but would not hear of it. I had, he said, enough responsibility already. He must bear his burden as best he could and face the issue manfully on his return to England. He thanked me for listening to him, but said that it would make it easier for him if we did not refer to the matter again. I promised, but with a lump in my throat, and vowed to myself that I would think less about my own troubles in future.

12

Not High Enough

Next morning saw the departure of Wish for Camp 3. After he had left I lay in my sleeping-bag thinking over his unhappy story. How strange, I thought, that all my companions – with the possible exception of Shute, with whom I had not yet had the opportunity to talk – had had such unexpected and melancholy experiences. How little one suspected of the secrets locked in the human breast! How seldom did one guess that the cheerful smile hid a breaking heart! This, I resolved, should be a lesson I would not forget: that we are all team-mates in suffering. I resolved that never again would I judge a person by his exterior, no matter how impenetrable or forbidding it might appear.

At that moment Pong entered with my breakfast. When I looked at his impenetrable exterior I realized that he, too, was just a human being, after all. Who knew what agony and desolation lay behind his flat and forbidding exterior? While suffering breakfast I thought about this. Had we, perhaps, been unkind to Pong? Poor fellow, he was the outcast of the expedition. Nobody seemed to like him. Was he, perhaps, intolerably lonely? Was he aching for a kind word or a smile?

It was almost too sad to think about. I put my breakfast aside and went to Pong's tent. I found him filing a fork into a bowl. He took no notice of me. After a while he laid down the fork and began to grate a piece of rock. I thought I had better let him get used to my presence before trying to communicate with him; so I sat down and watched him. After chopping up a portion of climbing rope and mincing an old sock he threw everything into a pan of pemmican stew and stirred for five minutes, adding sand and paraffin to taste. Finally, he strained it, spread some of it on a slice of leather, and took a hearty bite.

This, I thought, was my opportunity. Drawing his attention by a cough, I pointed to the leather and to my mouth.

At first he did not seem to grasp my meaning. I repeated the gesture, then made motions of mastication, smiled, and rubbed my stomach. His hand came slowly forward, as though he was still not sure what I wanted. I took the leather from him, bit off a small piece and returned it to him.

We chewed in silence. I let the situation consolidate itself for a few minutes, then I coughed again. To my great delight Pong coughed too! I turned one of his pans upside down and, with the point of a fork, drew on the dirty bottom a rough picture of a Yogistani fiancée. I pointed to Pong and to the drawing, and raised my eyebrows.

He didn't seem to understand. I kept on raising my eyebrows, and suddenly he started doing the same. He put his face quite close to mine and raised his eyebrows in time with my own.

I held my ground, and we went on like this for some time. I did not like to stop, fearing to hurt his feelings.

Then something strange happened to his face: something quite indescribable, like nothing I had ever seen before or imagined possible. I stared, fascinated. What could it be?

Then I knew. It was a smile!

I admit freely that I was touched. That Pong's forbidding exterior should break into a smile seemed almost like a miracle. What undreamed-of emotions could be the cause of it? With great eagerness I set about finding out.

I will not weary the reader with an account of the steps by which Pong and I developed our sign-language and came at last to understand each other. Such a thing might well seem impossible; but, as I have often had occasion to remark: good will is the best interpreter.

I told him about my family and described my home. I spoke warmly of our English cooking methods, and gave him one or two recipes. In return he showed me how to fry rubber, and told me that he was a graduate of the University of

Yogistan, where he had taken a third degree in cookery. At last, after some hours of persistence – for he had a tendency to chatter about trifles – I got him to tell me about his fiancée.

He had never wanted a fiancée. He had, he said, the artistic temperament, which he held to be incompatible with the sentiments and behaviour proper to one betrothed. He wished me to understand that he had nothing against the opposite sex – quite the contrary – but his artistic soul rebelled against the regimentation necessary to official engagement. Unfortunately, it is the Yogistani custom for children to be betrothed at an early age by parental arrangement. Thus, Pong was firmly engaged long before his artistic temperament showed itself, and when it finally did it found itself immediately at loggerheads with society, with his family and with his fiancée. Pong had always had a horror of loggerheads; his sensitive soul was intimately tuned to the most subtle nuances of social intercourse. Finding himself now at what appeared to be permanent and irreconcilable loggerheads with his fellow-creatures, in general and in the nearest particular, he underwent a spiritual crisis. As he saw it, he must choose once and for all between his art and his heart; he could be either an artist or a lover, but not both. The conflict was terrible. Pong told me that nobody could possibly have the slightest idea of what he went through. He had, until that time, been willing to accept his fiancée, and genuinely fond of his family and friends. Now, his deepest and most imperative urge was to abandon them all to follow the lonely path of his calling.

For months he lived in an agony of indecision. It seemed that his soul was being torn in two. Then one day something occurred which forced him to a decision. he was spending Saturday afternoon, as usual, at the home of his fiancée, who on these occasions was in the habit of preparing some special delicacy for her beloved. He sat down to table, grasped his chopsticks firmly in his right hand, placed his left hand on his hip, and assumed an expression of pleasant anticipation. The lady walked in proudly and placed a dish before him.

The next moment, Pong uttered a cry of horror and flung the bowl from him. The poor lady laid a hand on his arm, but he brushed her aside and rushed from the house.

All day and all night he paced the mountainside. In the morning he came down a changed – and a dedicated – man. From that morning he had devoted himself to his art. His fiancée, his family, his friends forsook him; he was uncompromising, and no one loved him sufficiently to understand and to accept second place in his affections. He became an outcast; not willingly or wilfully, for he was a sociable soul, but because the artist must tread his own unfrequented heights.

And as his skill increased and his insight sharpened, his desire for companionship increased also, until it was well-nigh intolerable. Yet the very strength of his longing was an added barrier between himself and his fellows; on the few occasions when he had revealed it the would-be friend had been appalled by its intensity. He became lonelier than ever.

At last he gave up the effort to reach his fellow-men. He retired completely into his inner world and poured all the vigour of his affections into his art. After taking his degree he made his own experiments and founded a new school of cookery which was acclaimed by the radical element throughout the country as the embodiment of the spirit of the age. He became universally respected and honoured, but never loved.

And now, he said, his life's work was done. He would never climb higher than he had already climbed. The rest would be mere repetition. Younger men must stand on his shoulders. For him, there remained gratitude to life for making use of him, the determination to grow old gracefully, and, deep and inextinguishable as ever, the human hope that he might yet find the affection of an equal.

★

That, if I understood him correctly, was Pong's story. For some minutes after he finished there was stillness in the little tent. Neither of us spoke a gesture. Then, with the sigh of one who returns to earth after an excursion into dreams, Pong drew out his pouch and offered me a pipeful of *stunk*. Too full for signs, I whispered a heartfelt: 'No thank you, old chap,' and hurried from the tent.

Back in my own tent I spat out the leather and got into my sleeping-bag. I lay a long time thinking about Pong's strange story and trying to imagine what the sign-language for 'maestro' might be. The expedition seemed very far away and everything connected with it strangely unreal. But at last I roused myself to a sense of my responsibilities. Where were the others? What should my own movements be?

A sharp twinge about the middle provided part of the answer. It was no use trying to pretend that I had no stomach-ache. A friendly Pong was not likely to be any more acceptable as a cook than he had been before. My dyspepsia tablets had run out. Unless help reached me soon I was lost.

I seized the walkie-talkie and buzzed. To my delight I made contact with Wish, who was at Camp 3. He had already been speaking to Constant and Shute, who had advanced to Camp 2. Burley and Jungle were still at Camp 1.

This was excellent news. The whole party could at last be united by radio. We soon discovered that I was out of range of Camp 2; I could speak to them only via Wish. Wish, likewise, could not reach Camp 1; his conversation with them must be relayed via Camp 2. I asked Wish to arrange for Constant to stand by at Camp 2 and Burley at Camp 1. While he was doing so I tried to make plans for the assault on the summit, still 7,000 feet above me. But the only plans I was able to make were connected with my stomach. I decided that dyspepsia tablets must be sent up at once, by porter, from the medical store at Camp 1.

When Wish called me again his voice was very faint, and I raised my own voice, asking him to speak up. Instead of doing so he became even fainter. I learnt afterwards that I was speaking too loudly and he, as one does in such cases, dropped his own voice instinctively. He was now almost inaudible to me, and I shouted as loudly as I could, which quite saturated his receiver and nearly deafened him. Neither of us could understand a word the other was saying. We might have given it up in despair had I not, while pausing to recover my breath, overheard Wish telling Constant that I was shouting his head off. This put me right, and soon Wish was able to tell me that they were all standing by.

But just as I was about to speak the radio began to crackle. From that moment we had the greatest difficulty in making ourselves understood. To make matters worse we forgot, in our enthusiasm, Jungle's careful training, and spoke as in ordinary conversation. The result was as follows:

MYSELF to Wish: Tell Burley to send six packets of number eights to Camp 4.

WISH to Constant: Tell Burley to send six packets of Weights to Camp 4.

MYSELF (who had overheard this): Not dates; *eights*.

WISH: I didn't say plates.

MYSELF: I didn't say you did.

CONSTANT to Wish: What do you mean, you didn't say crates? I know you didn't; you said packets.

WISH: No! No! I was talking to Binder. He says *not* dates. Or was it plates? Anyway, he doesn't want them.

MYSELF: But I *do* want them.

WISH to Constant: He says he does want them, after all.

CONSTANT: Wants what?

WISH: Why . . . er . . . just a minute! Binder: was it dates or plates?

MYSELF: Oh dear!

WISH to Constant: He says he wants some cold beer.

CONSTANT: Well, he knows we haven't got any. Is he light-headed, do you think?

MYSELF: *Not* beer! *Not* beer!

WISH to Constant: I think he must be. He says he wants some hot beer now.

CONSTANT: This is serious. He must be delirious. Ask him if he knows Burley.

WISH: Binder, Applecart wants to know if you rose early.

CONSTANT: Not Curly, you fool! *Burley.*

WISH: I didn't say Shirley.

MYSELF to Wish: I know you didn't.

CONSTANT to Wish: I didn't say you did.

WISH: WILL EVERYBODY PLEASE KEEP QUIET WHILE I GO GENTLY MAD.

BURLEY to Constant: What's going on, Applecart? Why are you talking nonsense?

CONSTANT: There's no wonder. Binder and Fiddler have gone off their heads.

BURLEY: Lost their beds?

CONSTANT: NO!

WISH to Constant: What on earth are you raving about? Can't you keep quiet while I try to think?

CONSTANT to Wish: If you want to think, turn off your ruddy receiver.

BURLEY to Constant: Who on earth wants to think? What *are* you talking about?

MYSELF to Wish: I didn't say anything. Are you sure you feel all right?

WISH: I FEEL AWFUL.

This was bad enough. But so far we had managed to synchronize our switching so that when A was speaking B was listening, and vice versa. Now we fell out of step. A and B would both be speaking and neither listening. Quite probably we were all speaking together at some time or other with nobody listening at all. For a long time it was chaos. I am sure that before very long we should have driven each other really mad, or at least that our faith in the rationality of human behaviour and man's control of his own destiny would have been seriously damaged. But we were spared this. Into our bedlam broke a voice: a lovely, controlled, pedantic, competent voice:

'Wanderer to Applecart. Wanderer to Applecart. Are you receiving me? Over. . . . Wanderer to Applecart. Wanderer to Applecart. Are you receiving me? Over. . . .'

Constant says that it came to him like the voice of a Superior Being. Through the crackling and distortion the familiar phrases rang clear and unmistakable. The monotonous chant which had seemed so strange when we rehearsed at Base Camp pushed like a bulldozer through the disturbance; the ear, not having to chase up and down, was able to ignore the interference. And the message left him in no doubt as to who was speaking to whom.

Constant took up the ritual joyfully:

'Applecart to Wanderer. Applecart to Wanderer. Receiving you loud and clear. . . .'

Wish, hearing him, put me right too, and our planning was soon proceeding smoothly. Burley promised to send off the number eights first thing in the morning. He and Jungle were uncertain as to their state of fitness and would remain at Camp 1 a little longer. Constant and Shute would stay at Camp 2 to rest after their climb. Wish would stay at Camp 3. This arrangement would keep open the radio contact. I decided that since the stomach tablets could not reach me before evening next day I might as well do a day's work while I was still strong enough to climb. I would go as high as I could, dump the equipment for Camp 5, and return to Camp 4.

★

I spent a restless night and rose unrested. Pong, when he brought my breakfast, was as inscrutable as ever, except that he allowed a powerful belch to escape him − a thing which had never occurred before. I wondered whether he had begun to take advantage of my sympathy; but rebuked myself immediately for the uncharitable thought.

When I summoned So Lo he, too, belched at me. This, if not a conspiracy, was a remarkable coincidence. I decided to keep my ears open in future. It is not pleasant to suspect that one has been taken advantage of. Apart from one's desire not to be thought a fool, or to think oneself one, one never knows whether to despise the other person for having taken mean advantage, or oneself for suspecting him without justification. It was with mixed feelings that I began the day's climb.

It was not long before my feelings were a good deal more mixed. I let So Lo take the lead as usual − it would, in fact, have been difficult to prevent him – and fell victim immediately to Binder's Butter Beans, which had attached themselves to the tune of 'Let Us With A Gladsome Mind' and were ten times as persistent as before. Besides fighting the Beans, I was trying to plan for the future. I was also trying to keep an eye open for warples and hallucinations and an ear for belches.

I was experiencing new and startling pains about the waistline, and the labour of climbing and breathing was getting more difficult. My mind began to wander. It seemed at one time that my companions had brought their fiancées and families with them; somewhere below me was a struggling crowd of people: Prone with his nasty wife and awful children, Burley and his unfortunate fiancée, Constant and Travers – singing sea-chanties – Jungle and his host of lost loves, and poor Wish with the fiancée he could not quite believe in. They were all my dear friends – even Prone's family – and I told myself I must make an effort for their sake. 'Come on, Binder!' I said to myself. But it was more easily said than done. It was no use trying to convince myself that I had no stomach-ache. My character was, I realized, already weakened by the lies I had told myself during the last climb. To deceive oneself was folly and cowardice. I must face up to the truth and accept it gladly. To accept truth was to accept life, and life itself would reward me.

So I started on my stomach-ache and tried to be

happy about it. Let my pain, I said, be my offering to life and to friendship. I would bear it happily for Pong's sake.

That sounded very nice, but it wouldn't work if I suspected Pong of taking advantage. For the sake of the expedition I must believe in Pong. After all, I told myself, Yogistani is spoken from the stomach; those belches might well be Yogistani for 'good-morning'.

So I put away my suspicions and tried to gather Pong and the others, and my stomach-ache, and all the rest of my troubles, into a single ecstasy. 'I will live!' I cried, and fell flat on my face.

I picked myself up and added a painful nose to my ecstasy. Aching with joy I forced myself on and up. And step by step the going became easier. I was thrilled to find myself climbing as I had not climbed for days. Had I found the secret of life and energy? The slope seemed barely perceptible; it was almost as though we were walking on level ground.

I raised my head and looked around me. We *were* on level ground!

I walked on a few steps and bumped into So Lo, who had stopped. I stood still, regaining my breath, then looked ahead, wondering what obstacles might be waiting for us.

To my utter astonishment, there were no obstacles.

We were on the summit!

For the second time on the expedition I doubted my own sanity. Rum Doodle was 40,000½ feet high. Unless either my barometer or myself was mad, we were at 35,000. What could have happened?

Then I saw. Over to the east a magnificent mountain stood against the sky, its glittering summit 5,000 feet above me.

We had climbed the wrong mountain.

13

It Goes!

Very small and lonely I felt as I shivered in the biting wind on the summit of North Doodle. The majestic summit of Rum Doodle towered above me, scarcely more than a mile distant; but between us the Conundra gorge plunged to awful and unseen depths.

My thoughts went back to that evening, which seemed an eternity ago, when we had stood on the summit of the Rankling La, our hearts beating with hope, eager to challenge the mountain. All the effort, the suffering, the planning, had been in vain. The confidence of those who had chosen us was betrayed. We were failures and frauds; the world would laugh at us, and rightly.

I thought of my comrades below, struggling against bodily weakness, building up their strength for the work which they imagined lay ahead, forcing their way up the mountain slowly but valiantly, and all to no purpose. It seemed infinitely pathetic. A lump rose in my throat and I fought back unmanly tears.

I looked up at the summit of Rum Doodle, so serene in its inviolate purity, and I had the fancy that the goddess of the mountain was looking down with scorn upon the puny creatures who had set sacrilegious feet upon her slopes, daring them to do their utmost, daring the whole world. She it was who had led us astray, and would lead astray or destroy all who set foot on her.

Would the mountain ever be climbed, I wondered.

And as I looked I had the answer.

On the broad slopes of the summit a small black speck had appeared. As I watched, it moved slowly upwards. Behind it came another speck. Then another.

Men!

Who could it be, upon our mountain? I felt a surge of indignation. Who had dared to come to the mountain in secret, to beat us to the summit and make fools of us? Who?

The three specks moved upwards. Behind them appeared other specks, in ones and twos and larger groups. There were ten of them, twenty, dozens, scores; the virgin whiteness of the summit snow was dotted with them. They swarmed all over it, like slow-moving ants.

The porters! It could be no one else. Ninety-two had been left at Base Camp. They must all, or nearly all, have climbed the mountain.

But why? Why?

And where was Prone? Was he with them, or had he been abandoned? Had he led them himself?

I seized my radio. The distance was beyond normal range, but contact might be possible in this clear air. I buzzed and called:

'Binder to Ailing. Binder to Ailing. Are you receiving me? Over.'

No reply. I tried again, and went on trying. I became frantic.

So Lo and Pong were seated placidly on their loads, smoking *stunk* and watching their friends on Rum Doodle with no sign of interest. It seemed to be all in a day's work to them. The specks on the summit were working in groups. Tents were being erected. They were evidently going to camp on the mountain top!

I went on calling.

At last, to my great relief, there came a faint voice:

'Ailing to Binder. Ailing to Binder. Receiving you strength 2. Are you receiving me? Over.'

And he told me his incredible story. On the day Constant and I left Advanced Base for the last time the porters had started to pack up all the equipment which we had left at Base Camp. When everything else was ready they pulled his tent down too and indicated by signs that he was to get out of his sleeping-bag. Assuming that they were carrying out Constant's orders to move the camp to a safer site, he did as requested, and they moved off in good order, Prone, who was suffering from suspected catalepsy, being carried by a porter on top of his load.

To his surprise, instead of making for the chosen site they marched straight to the North Wall and began to climb it. He shouted and wriggled, but the porter who was carrying him took not the slightest notice. He kicked and bellowed, and banged the fellow on the head with his fist. The man bore it for a while, then threw Prone off and went on alone. Greatly alarmed, Prone staggered after him, calling on him to stop. The porter halted, waited for Prone to come up, flung him over his shoulder and went on again. Prone, quite demoralized, made himself as comfortable as he could and fell asleep.

He awoke to find himself being carried into his tent. From a brief glimpse which he caught of the surroundings he guessed that they were encamped on the South Col. He was given food and his personal equipment was brought to him. After treating himself for Bavarian measles he turned in for the night.

Next morning they struck camp and Prone with it. Taking no notice whatsoever of his expostulations, the same porter threw him on top of his load, and off they went again.

And they kept hard at it, day after day, until they reached the summit. Prone said that he had never been so miserable in his life. The things he had endured, he said, would make a strong colonial turn pale by the mere telling. Rum Doodle was a far stiffer mountain than he had ever, in his most pessimistic moments, dreamed. He was carried all the way by the same porter, whose name was Un Sung.

I sympathized with him, and gave him my news. We then considered what was to be done. Obviously, Prone and the Base Camp must be got down the mountain. But how? At my suggestion Prone tried, by signs, to persuade his gang to go downhill, but they took no notice of him. They had by now finished pitching the tents. Those not engaged in preparing food were sitting inside smoking and apparently quite contented with their unusual situation. Prone said it was hopeless.

I said I could not imagine how the thing had happened. Prone said that he, on the other hand, knew exactly. The Yogistani word for mountain base was evidently the same as the word for summit, except for a grunt, gurgle or other internal convulsion which Constant had got wrong. In his opinion the porters would stay where they were until told by Constant to come down, or until supplies gave out. He expected to be dead long before either of these happened.

I begged him to bear up, for all our sakes. I told him that his sufferings had not been for nothing. Had we not, after all, reached the summit of Rum Doodle? We had, in fact, accomplished far more than we had set out to do, having climbed both Rum and North Doodle.

Prone said that, in years to come, if ever he sat again in comfort before a blazing fire, this fact might be of some small satisfaction to him. At present it was a raindrop in his ocean of misery. He begged me to get him off the mountain.

To comfort the poor fellow I promised that this would be done at once; though how, I had not the faintest idea. We said good-bye, and started down-hill with my small party.

★

At Camp 4 I found my precious packets of stomach tablets. I called up Wish and told him the news. I said I would go down to Camp 2 next day and Camp 1 the day after. I took a frugal supper and turned in early. So Lo and Pong both came and belched at me, and I hoped they were only saying 'good-night'.

It was a pair of belches which woke me next morning. I looked at them both suspiciously, but Pong had brought a piece of leather for me to eat with my lentils and pemmican. I took this to be a friendly gesture and was ashamed of my suspicions.

I can remember little of the next two days except my continual struggle with Binder's Butter Beans. At 27,000 feet I called up the others and asked them to direct me to Camp 1. They were very helpful, but their detailed instructions did nothing but lead me in a circle. But it was good to hear Burley's voice again. In the background, as he spoke, I could hear the sound of singing, and now and then someone would break into our conversation with a friendly enquiry, such as: 'How's old Binder today?' or 'Binder, old boy, did I ever tell you the story of the Young Lady from Kettering?' and so on. Burley himself offered to sing for me. It was very kind of them, and after my lonely journey I was touched; but it was no help to me in my search for Camp 1.

At last I gave it up. I said I would go down to Advanced Base, and asked them to follow next day. Burley consulted the others and I heard Shute say: 'We might as well; there's none left, anyway,' – meaning cinematograph film, I suppose.

I have since discussed with Totter the mystery of Camp 1. Why was I never able to find it, in spite of repeated instructions? Why had Constant been able to find it easily when he went down from Camp 2? And why did the others, notably Burley, who never went higher, find it so difficult to leave the camp? Was it a local climatic effect similar to the enervating air one often finds on a glacier? We never found a satisfactory explanation. To this day the mystery of Camp 1 remains unsolved.

So down I went to Advanced Base, and one day later we were all together for the first time for nearly a fortnight.

The question was: what was to be done about Prone? Jungle's telescope revealed that Base Camp was still pitched on the summit. A dark cloud which hung over it was doubtless the smoke from ninety-two pipes of *stunk*. Did they intend to stay there, as Prone feared, until ordered down or food ran out? Constant consulted the porters, who assured him that this was undoubtedly the case. Orders, they said, were orders; and these particular orders had been to take Base Camp to the summit and wait there for the rest of the expedition.

Clearly, someone would have to be sent after them. But who? Since none of the Europeans was fit to try we must send porters. Constant asked for volunteers, with disappointing results. He picked out two of them and ordered them up. After a haggle about overtime rates they packed their loads and set off at once without a sign of enthusiasm or reluctance. It was all in a day's work to them.

The South Col was no place for a group of tired mountaineers. Next day we descended to the glacier and set up our camp at the foot of the North Wall.

We waited.

14

Return of the Summit Party

We rested first, having our sleep out. Then, with returning energy, we became active again, each in his own way. Wish collated his many readings and announced with pride that they were proving of the greatest importance. Jungle was profitably employed in surveying the area. Unfortunately, he lost himself every day and had to be rescued at great inconvenience to the rest of us. This became so irksome that we appointed a porter to be his guardian, giving him strict instructions to bring Jungle back to camp at dusk. One evening they had not returned by nightfall and Shute sent up a number of flares – brought for photographic purposes – to guide them. One of the flares fell on Wish's tent and burnt it to the ground, together with his records. Wish was distracted. All his work had gone up in flames. Having boiled all the mercury out of his thermometers he could take no more readings, and the remainder of his equipment was on the summit of Rum Doodle. He had been unable to find any living creature on the mountain; this line of research also had come to nothing. There was only one hope of justifying his presence:

he must concentrate all his energies on the search for warples. Since Shute had no work of his own – all his film being spoiled and his lenses cracked – Wish conscripted him for the search. Burley was also enlisted. He was now fully acclimatized and as fit and active as a schoolboy, and fairly wore out both Wish and Shute on the daily warple-hunt.

Constant, insatiable as ever in his desire to improve his knowledge of the language, spent much time with the porters. At other times he was to be found wandering about the glacier practising grunts, gurgles and other phenomena which are the backbone of spoken Yogistani. It was the general opinion, he said, that Yogistani was unpronounce-able to the Western stomach, and it was his great ambition to prove that this was a fallacy. He was, he told me, within hearing of success. He had developed unmistakable symptoms of the perma-nent gastritis which is hypodermic amongst the Yogistani due to their speaking from the stomach. Burley was unkind enough to suggest that if Constant had developed his stomach-ache at the right time Prone would not now be marooned on the summit of Rum Doodle. I reminded him that but for this accident we would have failed in our purpose, and I congratulated Constant on his gastritis. It was, by the way, interesting to notice that as this complaint increased in severity Constant became more and more immune to the effects of Pong's cooking, and began even to enjoy it. He put forward the theory that the Yogistani method of cooking provides a counter-irritant to the indigenous indigestion pains. However that might be, it seemed to work in his case. It was unfortunate that on returning to civilization he found himself quite unable to stomach Western cooking. For weeks he lived on a starvation diet while he experimented with every conceivable mixture of ill-assorted foodstuffs and every possible method of rendering them indigestible. Finally, when on the verge of committing suicide by eating pre-digested invalid food, he conceived the happy idea of employing a Yogistani cook. He at once sent off cables in all directions, one of which, by great good fortune, reached Pong. Owing to the difficulty of transmitting grunts, gurgles and so on by cable, as well as to objections by Pong's trade union, the negotiations were prolonged, and Constant nearly succumbed to indigestion complicated by excitement. But matters were arranged at last. Pong is now installed in Constant's Hampstead flat. Almost any time of day they may be found grunting and gurgling together in the kitchen as they gloat over some malevolent mess which is burning on the bottom of a disgusting saucepan, or huddled in ecstasy over bowls of the same atrocity. When I last saw him Constant was smoking a pipe of *stunk*, which, he found, served the same purpose of counter-irritant as Pong's cooking.

But I anticipate. During this anxious time at

Base Camp, when the fate of poor Prone was as yet unknown to us, I was once more heartened and inspired by the devoted way in which my companions went about their tasks, allowing no personal grief to interfere with duty. I forced myself to take my part in all activities, social and otherwise, and found that in helping to lighten the burden of others I had also eased my own.

I had for some time been eager to learn something about Shute's fiancée; but now that opportunity presented itself I was at a loss how to broach the subject, not knowing what tender susceptibilities might be involved. One afternoon I was sitting alone in the mess tent, composing a letter of condolence for Prone's father, when Shute rolled in. He was, he said, at a loose end. Did I mind if he showed me some snaps? I said I should be delighted. He produced several photographs of a nice-looking young lady whom he said was his fiancée. They were to be married soon after his return. I congratulated him and wished him every happiness. He thanked me. I said that his fiancée looked a very nice young lady. He said she was the nicest and dearest person in the world. He told me quite a lot about her and it all sounded very happy and very normal. He asked me if he was boring me. I said no, but was there not some drawback to his happiness? He said no, why should there be? I said it often happened; perhaps he had had unhappy experiences before meeting his fiancée.

He said no; they had been childhood sweethearts; there had never been anyone else; why did I ask? I said that somehow I had expected something different. He looked at me rather suspiciously, I thought, and said he was sorry to disappoint me. I at once assured him that he had mistaken my meaning and asked him to tell me more, which he did, and more than satisfied my curiosity. His fiancée was evidently as normal and contented a person as he was himself; I could see that they would have a very happy life together. I asked him what they did on Saturday afternoons. He told me that they visited his fiancée's elderly aunt, who was bed-ridden.

I noticed that the daily belch with which Pong and So Lo greeted me on the mountain had spread to the other porters. I asked Constant if he knew what it meant. He said that since Yogistani was spoken from the stomach the belch – the stomach's sign of ultimate contentment – was used as an expression of respect; it indicated the great pleasure which the belcher found at being in the illustrious presence of the belchee.

This pleased me greatly, not only because I appreciated the honour, but because it confirmed my faith in Pong and in human nature. I wished that time and my duties would allow me to make friends with each of the porters. What a wealth of affection must, I thought, be hidden by their unresponsive manner. I spent much time with

Pong, who told me many interesting things about his life. Poor fellow, he seemed to have developed a great affection for me. He told Constant that I was the only person who had ever been kind to him without expecting something in return. This touched me deeply. He also developed a habit of bringing me little offerings of food at all hours of the day. This touched me deeply too.

★

After some days of careful thought I sent off the following despatch: 'Expedition more than success-ful, having climbed both Doodles. All in good health and spirits. The spirit of the team is excellent and the porters are beyond praise.'

I inadvertently signed this message 'Binder' instead of with my proper name. This caused some perplexity at home, and the despatch was at first considered to be a hoax. Then the rumour went round that we had been forestalled on the moun-tain by an unknown party under the leadership of one, Binder. Enquiries were made in mountaineer-ing circles, but no clue could be found. The affair caused considerable excitement, the national press making the most of it, and was not cleared up until our arrival at Chaikhosi, where we were inundated with telegrams from all parts of the world and had to employ three secretaries to deal with them. One of the secretaries turned out to be a practical joker named Pluke, who made the most of an unparal-leled opportunity and had the world's press at its wits' end by issuing foolish and contradictory statements. We had to employ six extra secretaries to clear up the confusion he caused.

But again I anticipate. As the days passed and no sign was seen of Prone I became more and more worried. Heaven alone knew what torments the poor fellow was enduring – if, indeed, he was still alive. At last I could stand it no longer. I called the others to the mess tent and said that something must be done. Someone must go up the mountain. The question was: who? All looked at each other, but no one spoke.

This made me feel very humble. 'My dear chaps,' I said, 'I know you all want to go; but someone must stay behind. I feel it my responsibility. I hope you won't consider it selfish if I go.'

There was silence. Then Burley looked at me keenly and said, in his deep voice: 'By heavens, Binder, I believe you would!'

I looked at him in surprise. He seemed, for some reason, to be overcome by emotion.

'If you go,' he said at last, 'I go!'

At that moment the tent door was flung open, and in walked Prone.

★

A new Prone.

An erect Prone.

A thin but healthy-looking Prone.

A Prone with a broad smile and a swagger.

Prone, the hero of Rum Doodle; the man who

had been higher than anyone else; for, as Wish pointed out, Prone stood head and shoulders higher than any of the porters.

What a reunion that was! What laughter! What back-slapping! What wrestling and practical jokes!

When we were all exhausted Prone said: 'As medical officer to this expedition I prescribe champagne. Where's the medical equipment?'

At this a silence fell upon us. The others looked sheepish and nudged each other to speak. At last, Burley said:

'The fact is, old boy, there *is* no champagne.'

'No champagne!' Prone was horrified.

'No. You see, we . . . er . . . didn't bring it back from Camp 1.'

But nothing could dampen our spirits that day. In the absence of a more stimulating beverage cocoa was made. We were soon laughing again, telling and retelling our adventures. Everybody wanted to talk, none to listen.

'Do you remember,' said Shute, smiling, 'how Binder got stuck to the glacier by his tears?'

'And had Pong all to himself for a week,' said Wish, chuckling.

'And couldn't find Camp 1,' laughed Jungle.

'And had to have number eights sent up,' added Constant, holding his sides.

We all roared.

All of a sudden, Burley jumped up.

'Stop it!' he cried.

He banged on the table.

The laughter stopped at once. The mood changed instantaneously. We waited in tense silence for Burley to speak. Wish giggled nervously, then coughed and turned red.

Burley was frowning. His fist thumped the table. He seemed to be struggling with words.

'There's something that needs saying,' he said at last. Then he fell silent again, and again we waited.

'A lot of things,' he continued, 'have happened on this expedition – and before it started – which seemed very appropriate at the time.'

He stopped again. He was evidently choosing his words carefully. He banged on the table. 'I wish now they had never happened.'

What on earth, I wondered, was the dear fellow talking about?

'I myself,' he was saying, 'have been as guilty as anyone else – probably more so.'

I noticed that the others were exchanging glances and looking sheepish again. What *was* it all about?

'Just now,' Burley went on, 'old Binder here was about to go to Prone's rescue. Let's not forget that. Let's not forget also that Binder had already done ten times as much work as the rest of us put together and carried the whole responsibility for the climb. He had already been to 35,000 feet while we were wallowing at Camp 1. Yet *he* was the chap who was going to climb Rum Doodle to bring Prone back.'

This was embarrassing. We had all done our best. I had perhaps been more fortunate than the others; but the luck might easily have been different. I tried to interrupt Burley, but he put his hand on my shoulder.

'No,' he said. 'Let me finish.'

He looked at the others, each in turn.

'I will now, gentlemen,' he said, 'propose the health of our leader: the most conscientious, the most modest, the most unselfish man I have ever climbed with.

'And,' he added, 'he has more guts than any of us.'

And those absurd fellows drank my health in cocoa.

The next moment they were all trying to shake my hand at the same time, while Prone was patting my back and saying: 'Well done, little man!'

It was quite ridiculous. To this day I am not sure whether it was another of Burley's feeble jokes.

15

Farewell to Rum Doodle

Next day we checked our stores and found that the porters had eaten nearly all the food, leaving only a few bags of butter beans. This was serious. We could not feed the porters another day; they must be dismissed at once. We decided to retain one porter only to carry our food for the return journey. We must abandon all our equipment, keeping only the most necessary personal effects, such as alarm clocks and hot-water bottles.

Constant addressed the porters and, after much excitement, told us that they understood the position. They insisted, however, on being paid up to the probable date of our arrival at Chaikhosi. Since to argue with them would mean feeding them for several days there seemed nothing else to do. We paid them and told them to be off. But instead of going they all came and stood in front of my tent, where I was cutting my toe nails. When I went out to see what they wanted, Bing came forward and stood in front of me. He looked me straight in the eye and uttered a powerful belch. Then he walked away. Bung followed him, then Bo, then So Lo and Lo Too; then all of them. One by one they came and belched at me. The glacier echoed with belches – from the deep bass rumble of Bing to the treble peeps of the boys. Burley said it reminded him of Aldershot. One little fellow seemed to be stomach-tied. He stood in front of me shyly, unable to produce a sound. Then he made a kind of cough and ran off amidst laughter.

Last of all came Pong. Poor fellow, the tears were streaming down his face. His magnificent belch brought a murmur of approval and admiration from all present. We embraced, and he pressed upon me a small black object, wizened and of indeterminate shape. I examined it, but could make nothing of it. I showed it to the others, who shook their heads.

Suddenly, Wish gave a great cry and snatched the thing out of my hand. It was a warple! A toasted and blackened warple; but still a warple!

Wish asked Constant to find out about it. Pong told him that the warple was considered a delicacy by the Yogistani. His kitchen hands gathered them every morning before breakfast.

Wish told Constant to offer *bohee* one for every warple brought to him. The porters immediately scattered in all directions, and soon started coming back with warples many, which they dropped at Wish's feet after receiving their money. Soon he had a pile some three feet high and was bankrupt. He appealed to Constant to stop them; but they went on until the district was denuded of warples.

Wish was now surrounded by a wall of warples and heavily in debt to the expedition.

The porters were now ready to depart. Being a punctilious race, they found it necessary to say good-bye all over again. Once more the glacier rang with belches. Once more Pong and I took an emotional farewell of each other. We little dreamed that we should meet again before many months were gone.

★

Next morning we made an early start. Wish had been up all night making a distillation of warple exegesis, which he carried in an exegesis bottle brought specially for the purpose. Burley had kindly stayed up to help him. Wish was overjoyed. His presence on the expedition had been justified, his fame assured. He was, he said, almost certain of an FRS.

Shute took the lead. He too had been up all night, helping Jungle to finish his map. Jungle had complained of fatigue in the morning and had drunk the spirit out of his compasses. As a result he had become slightly tipsy and had developed a tendency to face north, which caused him to walk sideways when going east or west and fall over backwards when going south. Owing to the path twisting in all directions his movements became remarkable. Shute helped him good-naturedly, but Wish, who was following, became so bewildered that he went quite giddy and fell on his hip, smashing his exegesis bottle. The contents ran down his legs and froze, so that he was stiff-legged for the rest of the day and fell down frequently. Burley spent the day picking him up and consoling him for his bruises and the loss of the exegesis.

Constant and Prone followed. Being deprived of Pong's cooking, Constant had been awake all night with stomach-ache. Prone sat up with him, worrying himself to death over his friend's condition. Constant was also very down at losing his porters. To comfort him Prone walked with him, his arm around his shoulders. Unfortunately, they both fell into a crevasse, but were rescued by the porter.

I brought up the rear. I was quite sad when I turned my back on the majestic stage where we had played our drama of suffering and triumph. When my companions broke into song with 'Binder's Butter Beans' I almost sobbed. But I comforted myself with the thought that our suffering was not yet over; and as I followed the happy and united party I was cheered by the reflection that our friendship had been tempered into bonds of steel by the perils we had faced together. I was tasting the keener rewards of leadership.

★

Three days later we stood on the summit of the Rankling La, facing the Rum Doodle massif for the last time. The evening sun had sunk below our horizon. The wilderness of mountains around us was a symphony in modulated shadow. Below was the utter blackness of river gorges. Only Rum Doodle itself stood in the sunshine, its great pyramid framed against a turquoise sky. The vast icy precipices and snowfields glowed with changing sunset tints.

It was a fitting farewell from a mighty mountain. Burley put his hand on my shoulder, and together we made our way through gathering darkness to our halting-place in the valley.

penguin.co.uk/vintage